JOSS

Touch the Sky

BY *Erin Falligant*

⭐ American Girl®

Illustrations and cover image by Maike Plenzke
Book design by Gretchen Becker

Cataloging-in-Publication Data available from the Library of Congress

americangirl.com/service

FOR MY CHEER TEAM,
ELIZABETH, JENNIFER,
DARCIE, AND KATIE,
WITH GRATITUDE

—E.F.

WiTH GRATiTuDe To:

Crystal da Silva, who holds multiple shortboard titles, including the 2007–2008 Sun Diego Surf Women's Pro-Am division, the 2009 World Deaf Surfing championship, and the 2014 US Open of Deaf Surfing: for being a guiding light for Joss's surfing experience.

Dr. Sharon Pajka, professor of English at Gallaudet University: for her invaluable insights regarding portrayals and perceptions of deaf characters in adolescent literature.

Julie Petersen and Sara Jo Moen, owners of Fury Athletics of Madison, Wisconsin, whose competitive cheer teams have won many prestigious competitions: for their guidance about all things cheer—including the bow!

Jennifer Richardson, AuD, educational audiologist and founder of Hearing Milestones: for her extensive contributions in matters of Joss's hearing loss, accommodations, communication, and social and emotional experiences.

Bianca Valenti, professional big-wave surfer and cofounder of the Committee for Equity in Women's Surfing: for her expertise in surf culture and for making the world of surfing a better place for all women and girls.

CONTENTS

The Spark
CHAPTER 1

Ba-DUM, ba-DUM, ba-DUM, ba-DUM . . . My heart kept time in my chest as I waited for my cheer team's turn to perform in the Shine Athletics gym. When the Mini team struck their final pose, the audience cheered—and my heart started beating double time. We were next.

This is it, I told myself. *The first time my family gets to see my cheer routine. My first chance to show what I can do!* I flapped my hands, trying to shake off my nervousness.

Beside me, Brooklyn bounced up and down. Her tiny black braids streamed like a fountain from the top of her sparkly cheer bow. "I'm freaking out, too," she said, talking a mile a minute. "But remember, it's only . . ."

The buzz of voices in the gym drowned out her last few words. "What?" I asked. I took a step closer so that I could watch her lips. I was born deaf in my left ear. I can hear with my right when I wear my hearing aid, but it's tough to catch every word in a loud place like the gym.

"It's only an exhibition show," she repeated, turning to face me. "That's just our families and friends out there."

~ 1 ~

"Yeah, it's not a real competition," added our teammate Mila. She sighed, her shoulders rising and falling.

Part of me was glad we had the chance to practice our routine in front of our friends and families. But the other part of me wished, like Mila, that this showcase were a real competition—that we didn't have to wait another five weeks until the SoCal Spirit Challenge. Our Junior Level One team had been practicing nonstop. If there were a trophy to win today, we'd take it home for sure.

I decided to pretend there *was* a trophy—and that I wasn't the least bit nervous. *Never let them see you sweat.* That's what I tell myself when I'm surfing a big wave or trying a new trick at the Break, my favorite surf spot here in Huntington Beach.

When someone tapped my shoulder, I whirled around. "Reina!"

Reina is on the Senior cheer team and helps coach our Junior One team. She's an amazing flyer, the person at the top of stunts and pyramids. She also happens to be dating my oldest brother, Liam, which means I get to see her a lot outside the cheer gym, too.

As Reina leaned down for a hug, her dark ponytail brushed across my face, smelling sweet and citrusy.

"Ready?" she signed in American Sign Language, or ASL.

"Ready!" I said, flashing my most confident smile. "Fake it till you feel it, right?"

Reina grinned. During cheer tryouts last spring, she'd taught me that *acting* confident can actually help me *feel* more sure of myself. "Attagirl," she said. "Team Shine cheer?"

She held out her hand, palm down. I grinned and slapped mine on top of hers. Then Brooklyn and curly-haired Cassie joined us, and Mila, too. When all eight girls on the Junior One team had joined the circle, we started wiggling our fingers.

"Shhhhhhh . . ." We raised our fluttering fingers into the air. When our hands were high overhead, we spread our fingers wide and shouted, "Shine!"

Reina laughed. "You're ready, all right." She turned back toward Coach Kara, waiting for her to finish introducing my team to the audience. At last, Reina waved us onto the mat.

As I smiled at the crowd, I felt another rush of nervous energy. Half of the gym had been taken over by folding chairs, and my family sat front and center. Mom signed "good luck" in ASL, Dad waved, and Liam gave me a thumbs-up.

My other brother, Dylan, was getting ready to film our performance, his phone raised in the air. Wait . . . no he wasn't! As he held the back of his phone to his mouth, huge cartoon lips appeared on the screen.

Argh. Classic Dylan, always goofing around. But I wasn't going to let him mess me up.

When my best friend, Sofia, popped up from the seat behind Dylan, I barely recognized her. Her shiny black hair was pulled up into a huge cheer bow. She wiggled her head, just in case I'd somehow missed the bow. *Ha!*

Sofia is my Surf Sister. We spend hours surfing together at the Break. She was surprised when I first decided to join cheer. But now that she knows how much I love it, she's been supporting me—one hundred percent.

I shot Sofia a grateful smile and took my place on the mat. As I waited for Coach Kara's count, our music burst from the speakers. To me, it was just a blur of noise, but then I heard Coach's voice—"Five, six, seven, eight"—sent straight to my hearing aid from the microphone she wore on a cord around her neck. She held up her fingers, too, just to be sure I was ready.

I sprang into action, cartwheeling across the mat alongside my teammates. I rocked the tumbling sequence, nailing my roundoffs and back walkovers. Only a few months ago, I'd needed a spotter for those walkovers. But not anymore! Reina had helped me master them.

When it was time to show off our jumps, I hit them all. Every. Single. One. Three toe touches in a row. My legs were strong from surfing and from months of practicing on the trampoline.

Then I cartwheeled toward my stunt group. Brooklyn and I faced each other as sturdy bases, and Mila put her hands on our shoulders. As she jumped, we caught her feet in our hands. Cassie spotted from behind, grabbing Mila's ankles. On the next count, we dipped down slightly and then hoisted Mila up into an elevator. We kept her feet steady at shoulder level as she stood straight and tall.

Next to us, our other stunt group hit their trick, too. Lauren, their flyer, did a lib, short for "liberty." She stood above her base group on one foot and lifted her other knee. She held one arm overhead, like the Statue of Liberty. Her other arm was locked with Mila's, combining our group into a pyramid.

When the crowd went crazy, my chest pounded with pride. On the next eight count, we popped Mila up a little higher and she kicked her legs out in front of her. We caught her in a cradle and released her back onto the mat.

Then it was time for the final dance routine. *This one's for you, Sofia,* I thought with a grin. She's a better dancer

than I am, and she'd been teaching me how to keep my
moves sharp and snappy. By the time the music ended,
I was beaming from ear to ear. I did it!

Sofia and my family waved their hands in the air,
a cheer that I could see instead of hear in the noisy gym.
Even Dylan pointed at his phone and gave me a thumbs-up.
I guess Mr. Cartoon Lips had filmed my routine after all.

Coach Kara waved us off the mat with high fives and
a smile. Then she hurried toward the Junior Two team.
We sat down by the mat to cheer them on. Just as I'd been
reminding Dylan all summer, All Star cheerleaders don't
stand on the sidelines cheering for football or basketball
teams. We're a sport and a team of our own. But we sure do
a lot of cheering for each other!

As I sat beside Brooklyn, Reina knelt in front of us.
"Great job, girls!" she said, giving us fist bumps. "Your team
looks amazing. You might be the first Shine Athletics Junior
One team to win the SoCal Spirit Challenge since . . ."

"Shhh . . . Shine!" The Junior Two girls did their Team
Shine cheer, swallowing up Reina's last words.

"Since *when*?" I asked.

Brooklyn faced me. "Since Reina was on the Junior One
team!" she said, her brown eyes dancing.

It was hard to imagine that Reina was ever on Junior
One. She'd been on the Senior team since I'd first met her

a couple of years ago, and they'd won nationals the last two
years in a row!

"I think you girls can do it," Reina said with a smile.
"You have the confidence to win." She looked straight at
me when she said that part. "And if you do win, Coach says
your team can celebrate with a sleepover in the gym, with
me and some of the other senior girls. What do you say?"

A sleepover in the gym? With the senior cheerleaders?
"I'm in!" I said, before any of my teammates could respond.

As Reina jogged back to her own team, Brooklyn nudged
my shoulder. "We can sleep on the panel mats!" She pointed
to the folded-up mats pushed up against the wall.

I pictured our sleeping bags side by side on those cushy
mats. "Yes! Great idea."

Mila leaned around Brooklyn. "I call dibs on the trampoline!"

Brooklyn shot her an envious look. "No fair! You have
to share."

Mila shrugged. "Maybe I will, maybe I won't." She
grinned.

For just a moment, I closed my eyes, picturing the gym
at night: Mats covered with sleeping bags. Twinkly lights
overhead. Hanging out with with my teammates—and
Reina—all night long!

Suddenly, I wanted to win that competition in October

more than ever. What had started as a spark in my chest was a full-on flame now. We *had* to win the SoCal Spirit Challenge—to make Reina proud and to earn that sleepover.

You have the confidence to win, Reina had said to us. To *me*.

I didn't have to fake it anymore—this time I really felt it. Yep, "confidence" was my new middle name. Jocelyn "Confidence" Kendrick was going to do whatever it took to win.

Ramping Up

◜ CHAPTER 2 ◞

*N*ever *let them see you sweat.* Those words had gotten me through our exhibition performance at cheer yesterday. And it's what I told myself again on Sunday afternoon when I caught my first big wave at the Break.

As I zoomed down the face of the wave, butterflies fluttered in my belly. I *live* for moments like this, when I can feel the energy of the water beneath my board—my beautiful, new, light-as-a-feather board.

I'd won it over the summer in a surf video contest I'd entered with Sofia, Dylan, and his buddy Nico. We'd also won a surf session with pro surfer Tina Hart, who happens to be my idol. *Best day of my life*, I thought. Because that was also the day when I'd finally landed the frontside air, an aerial trick I'd been working on for forever.

Could I pull off another frontside air today? I'd tried twice already. Maybe the third time would be the charm. I hit the bottom of the wave and then turned and pumped back up. Airs are all about confidence, so I gave myself a quick pep talk: *Prepare to fly. Touch the sky.*

As I neared the lip of the wave, I kicked the tail of

my board down and felt the nose of the board lift up. My stomach dropped, but once you commit to an air, there's no backing down. You've got to be all in, one hundred percent—that's what Tina Hart had taught me.

So I tucked my knees to my chest, just like when I do a tuck jump in cheer. Quick as lightning, I grabbed the rail, or side of my board, and scoped out my landing. Then I snapped my legs back down. As my board slid down the face of the wave, a jolt of energy ran from my head to my toes. *Yes!*

Nothing feels better than landing a frontside air. *I'll never get used to it*, I told myself. *Even if I'm a pro surfer like Tina Hart someday, that trick will never ever get old.*

I rode the wave back to shore and jogged out of the water to my beach towel. Sofia, Dylan, and Nico were already sprawled on the sand, air-drying under the warm mid-September sun. As I plopped down beside my Surf Sister, she offered me a fist bump. "Nice wave!" she signed in ASL.

Then Dylan tapped my head, his annoying way of getting my attention. "Killer trick," he signed when I turned around. "You can really rip!"

A compliment from Dylan? Heat rose to my cheeks, but I grinned and signed, "Thanks." After I'd dried my ear and put my hearing aid back in, I spun to face him. "So if I'm such a ripper, why won't you take me to Shadow Rock?"

Even saying the name out loud gave me chills. Shadow Rock was Dylan's new Saturday morning surf spot, a break with huge waves—the kind he likes to tackle. I hadn't surfed it yet. But I'd been bugging Dylan for weeks to take me and Sofia with him.

Dylan's eyes narrowed. "Give it up, Joss," he said, signing as he spoke. "The answer's still no."

"C'mon, Dylan!"

He held up his hand. "I'm only saving you from yourself. Those waves will crush you like a bug." He smacked the top of one hand with the other and then pretended to flick away a squished bug.

I rolled my eyes. "I think I can handle it."

Sofia threw her arm around my shoulders. "You can," she said. "Everyone knows it—even Dylan." She shot him a look. "But right now, we've gotta go or we'll be late for Brooklyn."

I checked the time on my phone. 1:33. *Yikes!* Brooklyn was meeting us at my house at two o'clock. I tugged my board shorts on over my swimsuit.

Sofia and I packed up our boards and raced past the lifeguard stand toward the SoCal Board Shop. Sofia's mom owns the shop, and she lets us leave our boards in the back so we don't have to carry them home on our bikes.

As we locked up our boards on the rack, I kept picturing those big waves at Shadow Rock. I'd mastered the frontside air—well, I could land it anyway. So why did Dylan think I couldn't handle a few big waves?

Brooklyn's bike was already in the driveway when we got to my house. "Dad is probably talking her ear off in the garage," I told Sofia as I pulled off my helmet. Dad is always working on some woodworking project, and he loves to have company.

But the garage was empty—really empty, as if Dad had hauled all his stacks of wood to the dump or something. As I led Sofia to the backyard, I realized why.

A wooden ramp sat in the middle of the yard—a skate ramp. Dad had built two fly ramps and pushed them together to form a perfect half circle. And that ramp was practically begging me to grab a skateboard and try it out.

"Surprise!" Dad shouted. Brooklyn stood beside him with a ginormous smile.

As Sofia ran to greet Brooklyn, I grabbed a skateboard from the bin just inside the garage. Then I raced toward the ramp, stopping only long enough to give Dad a hug.

"What do you think?" he asked, running his hand

over his shaved head. "Big enough to do a few airs? Or even a three-sixty?" He winked.

I laughed. Liam could do three-sixties on a surfboard, spinning a full circle in the air before landing back on a wave. But it'd be tough to do a three-sixty on a small skateboard ramp, even for a ripper like Liam.

Could I land a few smaller skate tricks on it, though? I couldn't wait to find out. I stepped onto my skateboard and pushed up one side of the ramp, savoring the smoothness of the wood beneath my wheels.

As I rolled back down, I pumped my legs to build some speed. I carved back and forth a few times. Then I zoomed up one side of the ramp and did the smallest of ollies, kicking up the nose of the board until my wheels left the ramp. My timing was way off, though. As I spun my board back toward the ramp, I biffed my landing and slid down the ramp on my butt.

I laughed and hopped off the ramp. "Your turn, Sof. You're the one with the sick ramp skills. Show us what you've got!"

She stood up and brushed off her Hawaiian-print shorts. Sofia's skate tricks are as creative as her outfits. She's great at combining lip tricks, the ones done at the top of the ramp.

Before I could even take a seat, she sailed up one side, rolled onto the lip, and dropped back down. On the other

side, she pressed down the tail of
her board, like popping a wheelie
on a bike.

"Go, Sofia!" cheered Brooklyn.

I tried to whistle on two fingers like Dylan does, but nothing
came out. So I clapped instead.

By the time Sofia hopped off her board,
her nose glistened with sweat.

"You're both so good!" said Brooklyn.

I sighed. "I'm a better surfer than a skateboarder,"
I admitted.

"No kidding," Sofia teased. "Too bad you can't show
off your frontside air in the school talent show."

The talent show was only a few weeks away. Sofia and
I had been trying to come up with an act for what felt like
forever. Next year, we'd be in middle school, so this was
our last chance to win at Fountain Valley Elementary—our
last chance to get our photos on the Wall of Fame, like both
my brothers did when they were fifth-graders.

"If only there was a way to bring the ocean to school,"
I mused, laughing out loud as I imagined the auditorium
flooded with water. "Yeah, I don't think a surfing act is going
to work."

Sofia shrugged. "Oh, well. A girl can dream."

Brooklyn laughed. "A surf act would be tough to pull off. But skating looks a lot like surfing, at least to me!"

That gave me an idea. "What if we could do a 'surfing act' for the talent show?" I asked, curling my fingers into air quotes. "Could we decorate the ramp to look like a wave?"

Sofia, who is pretty much the best artist I know, took my idea and ran with it. "Totally!" she said. "We could paint it ocean blue and add a few swirls on the side to make it look like white water. Wait," she said, grabbing my hand, "do you mean take the ramp to school? For the talent show? Like a surf-skate act?"

I nodded. "We'd win the talent show for sure with your tricks and that ramp!"

"Yes!" Sofia's eyes danced. We did our fist-bump routine: fist bump, butt bump, another butt bump, and then a fist-bump finger explosion.

I shot a guilty glance at Brooklyn. I hated to leave her out. "Do you want to skate with us in the talent show?" I asked.

Brooklyn shook her head so hard that her braids slapped against her face. "No way. No one wants to see me on a skateboard—it's not pretty. But maybe I can help you paint the ramp."

"You could!" said Sofia. "I mean, you were the one who

inspired the whole idea." She gave Brooklyn a fist bump, then a couple of butt bumps, and then . . . she added a *cheer bow*. She signed the word *bow* in ASL, crossing her hands in an X on top of her head and pointing her index and middle fingers outward. Ha! Leave it to Sofia to take something good and make it even better.

She held out the skateboard. "Are you sure you don't want a turn?"

Before Brooklyn could answer, I saw a flash of white. Murph, my family's English bulldog, lunged toward the skateboard and grabbed it in her mouth. She waddled away, dragging the board toward the garage. Dad, who had just let Murph out the back door, waved and signed, "Sorry."

Brooklyn whirled around to face me. "Where's she taking that skateboard?"

I grinned. "C'mon, I'll show you."

Murph was already in the driveway when we caught up with her. Then she dropped the board and climbed onto it, pushing off with a paw.

She's goofy-footed like me, which means we push with our left paws—er, feet. And Murph can get some speed, but she doesn't always skate the straightest path. When she hit the edge of the driveway, she tumbled off. But she dragged her board right back up the driveway and got back on.

Brooklyn laughed so hard that she got the hiccups. "That's adorable," she said. "She's so determined!"

"She is," I said, feeling a flush of pride. *Just like me,* I thought. *When I set my mind to something, I do it. Like winning the SoCal Spirit Challenge. And the talent show.*

Could my friends and I somehow do both?

Team Fury

On Monday night, I carried that determination with me into cheer practice. I headed straight for the trampoline to work on my back handsprings. I couldn't do them on my own yet, but I could practice them using the spotting rig harness.

Is Mila ever going to be done with her turn? I wondered, glancing up at the ropes suspended from the ceiling. She was using the spotting rig to practice back tucks, not handsprings. When it came to tumbling, Mila was always a step ahead of everyone else.

Beside me, Brooklyn waved to get my attention. "Maybe I'll sleep here during the sleepover," she said, pretending to take a snooze on the wedge mat, which looked like a giant hunk of cheese. She started sliding slowly downhill.

"Only if you want to end up on the floor by morning," I said, laughing.

When I turned back around, Mila was climbing off the tramp—finally. She stepped toward us. "You know, there won't even be a sleepover unless we beat Team Fury," she said.

"Who?" I asked.

Brooklyn hopped up to explain. "Fury Athletics is the other cheer gym in Huntington Beach. Team Fury is our top rival in the SoCal Spirit Challenge."

"Their stunts are amazing, and they get better every year," said Mila. "So we're going to have to rock our own stunts in that competition."

"We will," I said. "With you and Lauren as our superstar flyers, we'll win hands down."

Mila gave me a high five and then jogged toward a group of girls who were practicing tumbling.

After I climbed onto the tramp, I put on the spotting rig belt and adjusted my headband. It keeps my hair out of my face and holds my hearing aid in place. I did three handsprings in a row and then steadied myself, waiting for the walls around me to stop swirling. Across the gym, I saw Reina towering over her teammates from the top of a pyramid.

What would it feel like to be a flyer like Reina? I wondered.

As my eyes flickered back to my own team, I saw Mila showing off her back handsprings. Wow, she was really flying! But out of the corner of my eye, I saw someone else cartwheeling from the other direction—in a crooked line. *Lauren.*

I wanted to holler at them to stop, but it was too late!

Lauren launched into one final cartwheel, and a split second later, the two girls collided.

Mila rolled and popped back up on her feet, but Lauren hit the mat hard. When she sat up, she was holding her ankle, and tears streamed down her face.

Coach Kara was beside her in a flash. Mila rushed over, too. I kept hoping Lauren would hop back up and say, "I'm good, no worries. Take two!" But she didn't. When Coach Kara finally helped Lauren off the mat, she was limping.

A few minutes later, when Coach asked us to move on to the dance portion of our routine, I waited for Lauren to join us. Mila kept shooting her guilty glances, too.

I was so busy worrying about Lauren that I missed Coach Kara's count—twice. She finally waved a hand at me. "Pay attention, Joss," she said into her microphone.

I tried, I really did. But why was Reina bringing Lauren another ice pack?

Our whole team kept getting distracted, so Coach finally gave us a water break. Brooklyn and I grabbed our water bottles and sat down next to Lauren.

"Reina thinks I might have sprained it," Lauren said tearfully. When she lifted the ice pack to show us her ankle,

I sucked in my breath. It was swollen and turning three shades of purple.

"Are you going to be okay?" Brooklyn asked.

She shrugged. "I don't know."

"I'm sure you'll be back on your feet by tomorrow," I said, trying to sound cheerful. But my stomach churned.

Lauren was our best flyer. We needed her to do the pyramid at the end of our cheer routine. If Team Fury kept upping their stunt game, we needed to do our best stunts, too.

But how could we do our best without our best flyer?

Friday morning before school, Sofia dragged Brooklyn and me down the hall toward the Wall of Fame. "For inspiration," she said.

The wall was decorated with photos of all the past talent show winners. Right away, I spotted Liam with his skateboard. It was weird to imagine my big brother as a fifth-grader. But there he was, about two feet shorter than he is now, with skinny arms and a crooked smile.

Dylan's goofy face stood out a few photos away. He was wearing a magician's hat. Next to him, Nico wore rabbit ears. Sofia nudged my shoulder. "Does Dylan still do those magic tricks?" she asked.

"Nah. His magic show was more like a comedy act, remember? He and Nico were total goofballs onstage." I might do anything to win, but Dylan would do anything for a laugh.

Brooklyn cracked up just looking at the photo, until red-headed Annika walked up beside us. She was in the other fifth-grade class. I didn't know her well, but Brooklyn must have, because her smile disappeared. "What's up, Annika?" she asked.

"Just checking out the talent show rules," said Annika. "Some of us from Team Fury are doing a [*squeak, squeak, squeak*]."

A kid wearing sneakers jogged by, making it tough to hear Annika. But I'd caught the two most important words: *Team Fury*. Annika was on the other cheer team in town— our rivals for the SoCal Spirit Challenge!

Annika leaned against the wall. "I heard Team Shine is down a flyer. Is she going to recover in time for the cheer competition?"

"Yep," said Brooklyn. "I'm not worried."

I knew *that* wasn't true. Lauren had sat out at practice all week, and our whole team was nervous about what it might mean. But Brooklyn wasn't going to let Annika see her sweat.

"That's good," Annika said a little too sweetly. She crossed her arms. "So are you doing cheer for the talent show?"

Sofia opened her mouth to answer, but Brooklyn jumped in. "We're skateboarding," she said.

We?

Sofia caught my eye and raised an eyebrow.

"I mean, Joss and Sofia are skateboarding. They're really good. Joss's dad built a . . ." Brooklyn started talking so fast that I missed half her words. "And you should see Joss's dog ride a . . . She could win the talent show all by herself!"

Annika's cheeks turned pink. "Your dog is going to be in the talent show?"

Brooklyn turned toward me, pleading with her eyes.

"Maybe," I said casually, playing along. "I mean, who knows? She might."

Annika's face tightened. As she hurried away, Brooklyn blew out her breath. "Thank you," she said. "Annika tries to psych me out whenever competition season comes around. But this year, I'm not gonna let her."

"Who is Team Fury?" asked Sofia.

"Only the toughest Junior One cheer team around," said Brooklyn. "They win the SoCal Spirit Challenge every year. At least, every year since Reina's team won."

"Every year?" I asked, wondering if I'd heard her right.

"Every year."

Sofia bit her lip. "That means their talent show act is going to be pretty good, too."

"Not better than Murph, the Amazing Skateboarding Dog!" said Brooklyn. "Right?"

"Slow down, guys," I said. "I mean, Murph can skate the driveway all day, but she'd rather nap on the skate ramp than ride it! Besides, we don't even know if Principal Harris will allow dogs in the talent show."

Sofia shrugged. "She let Greyson Lewis bring his dancing Chihuahua last year, remember? So we should at least try to teach Murph how to ride the ramp."

I took a deep breath. "I guess we have to now. If Team Fury is as good as you say they are, we might need Murph in order to win."

Brooklyn turned to face me. "I sure hope Murph is a fast learner," she said, holding her math book tight to her chest. "The talent show is less than two weeks away."

The next day, as Mom, Sofia, and I finished our lunch at Jo-Jo's Café, we watched beachgoers heading toward the pier. We couldn't see the ocean from the café patio on Main Street, but we could smell the salt water and seaweed.

Sofia blew her bangs off her forehead. "Are Dylan and Liam surfing at Shadow Rock right now?" she asked me.

I sighed. "Yep. They go every Saturday."

I started to go off about how Dylan thought I couldn't handle the waves at Shadow Rock, but then Mom nudged my shoulder. "Look who's here," she said.

I did a double take. A woman with a reddish-brown ponytail was walking toward our table. Coach Kara? I'd never seen her outside the gym before. It felt so weird!

She waved at me. "Hi, Joss!"

"Oh, hey!" I waved back.

Coach didn't waste any time getting down to business. "I'm glad I ran into you. I've been wanting to talk to you about Lauren," she said.

When Mom offered Coach a chair, she took it.

"Lauren suffered a pretty bad ankle sprain and will be in a boot for a while. She won't be able to practice again for four to six weeks."

"Four to six weeks?" I blurted. "But our competition is only a month away!"

"That's right," said Coach Kara. "So I'd like to talk to your team about making some changes to your stunt groups—maybe moving Mila over to Lauren's stunt group."

My jaw dropped. Mila was part of *my* stunt group. "Who would be our flyer then?" I asked.

The next words out of my coach's mouth caught me off guard. "Joss, I'd like you to try that spot."

Huh?

She spoke again, as if she thought I hadn't heard. "Are you interested in being a flyer, Joss?"

A flyer? Like Reina?

My brain finally caught up, and the answer popped right out of my mouth. "Yes!"

"You're a strong athlete," said Coach Kara. "I think you could fly tight, keeping your body straight and strong, like Mila does. And you're flexible. We've seen that with your jumps, right?"

"Yes!"

"And you have good balance—probably from all that surfing." She winked at me.

"Yes!" That seemed to be the only word I could come up with.

"You're not afraid of heights, are you?"

"Yes! I mean, no. Wait, what was the question?"

Luckily, Sofia was sitting beside me. "Nope, she's fearless," she declared.

I blushed and gave my Surf Sister a grateful smile.

"Good," said Coach Kara. "But you'll need to come to . . . on Thursdays." As a chatty group of kids biked past, I struggled to make out Coach's words.

"To what?" I studied her face.

"A flyer class on Thursdays," said Mom, signing as she spoke. "And yes, you have my permission." She was smiling so wide that I thought her face might burst.

"I'll go to the class!" I said to Coach, finally finding my voice. "I'll do whatever it takes to help our team win the competition in October."

"Great!" said Coach Kara. "I'm glad to hear it, Joss. We'll see how you do over the next couple of weeks, okay?"

As she pushed away from the table, I felt that familiar rush of excitement and nervousness, like I do whenever I try a new surf trick or surf a really big wave.

Except this time, wiping out wasn't an option. Not when my whole team was counting on me!

WOBBLY LEGS

☾ CHAPTER 4 ☽

On Thursday night, I showed up at the gym an hour before regular practice. I felt like Brooklyn, bouncing with nervous energy! But she wasn't here to help me burn it off. This class was for flyers only.

I glanced around the gym. I recognized Owen, because he's one of only three boys at Shine Athletics and one of the best flyers. The only other person I knew was Mila, who was showing off a perfect scorpion. She stood on one foot and pulled her other foot up behind her with both hands. When she saw me, she let go of her foot and waved.

"Bummer about Lauren, right?" she said.

I nodded.

"I guess I get to do the lib now," she said, perking right back up. "As long as you can do the [*whoosh!*] . . ."

I strained to hear as Coach Kara slid a folded mat across the floor. "The elevator?" I asked, stepping closer to Mila. "I can do it—I mean I'll learn how. We still have a month."

She chewed her lip. "More like three weeks."

Sheesh. No pressure there, I thought to myself. "Don't worry, Mila. I'll learn the stunt."

She stared at me as if she wasn't so sure. I knew Mila could be competitive. When I'd first met her at cheer tryouts, she didn't seem to want a surfer girl like me on her cheer team. But eventually, she had learned to trust me. Or so I thought . . .

I was relieved when Reina walked over. "Hey, flyers," she said. "You ready for this?"

"I'm ready," I said, talking fast like Brooklyn does when she's nervous. "Which stunt will we start with? The elevator? Or the lib?"

Reina smiled. "Neither. Coach always starts class with stretching, and then you'll practice body positions. Remember, flyer class is about flexibility and *practicing* flying tight."

"Oh, right." *Prepare to fly,* I reminded myself. That's what I was doing here.

Reina nodded in Coach Kara's direction "Looks like we're about to get started. Why don't you two partner up?"

I wasn't crazy about that idea—Mila was kind of stressing me out right now. But I mustered a smile and stepped toward her.

I'm pretty strong from swimming and surfing. But during the first few stretches, Mila's legs seemed a whole lot bendier than mine. As she leaned against the wall, I helped her stretch each leg out behind her. She didn't need much help—her foot rose nearly to my shoulder.

When it was my turn, she leaned around my leg and asked, "Is that really the highest you can go?"

I managed to lift my foot an inch higher, but my leg started to shake.

The stretching part of class dragged on forever. When it was finally time to move on, Mila jogged over to a row of stunt stands. She stepped onto the small platform, as if balancing on a fence post. As I hustled over to the stand next to Mila's, Coach Kara's voice rang out in my ear.

"Why don't you start on a panel mat, Joss? It'll help you get the feel of stepping up and flying tight." She pushed a folded-up mat toward me. It wasn't even a foot high. How would I learn to fly high just a few inches off the ground?

When I saw another girl using a mat, I felt better. At least I wasn't the only beginner working on a "baby mat" tonight.

And I won't be on it for long, I promised myself.

Coach clapped her hands. "All right, flyers. Let's start with the lib."

Mila didn't even wait for Coach's cues. She balanced with one foot on her stunt stand and raised her other knee in the air, her arms high overhead.

"Remember," said Coach, "as you step up with your right foot, lock that standing leg.

Tighten your body as you raise the other knee. Bend, one, two, lock, three, four . . ."

As I stepped onto the panel mat, Mila towered over me from her perch on the stunt stand.

Don't worry about her, I told myself. I straightened my right leg and pulled in all my muscles. But I felt so unsteady with my knee locked. When I surf, I bend my knees for stability. How was I supposed to balance on this squishy mat without bending my knee?

Somehow, I managed to stay upright. On Coach's five count, we put our hands up in a high V. On seven, we lifted one knee up into a lib. I wobbled, but Mila stayed perfectly steady.

After the lib, we moved on to the heel stretch, balancing on one leg and kicking the other foot forward into one hand. When I straightened my leg, my hand didn't quite reach my foot, so I grabbed my ankle instead. I locked my standing leg and kept my balance. Barely.

When Reina came to check on me, I nearly lost my balance—but recovered just in time.

"When are we moving on to elevators?" I asked her, ready to leave the lib behind.

She laughed, her brown eyes twinkling. "Two-legged stunts are easier to work on in regular practice with your stunt group," she said. "Patience, Joss. Try to focus on what you're doing right now."

I smiled and tried to lift my leg a little higher, but I had to let go when I nearly fell over. *After the lib and the heel stretch, an elevator will seem easy*, I told myself. *I'll be towering over my teammates on two legs instead of one.*

When I glanced at the clock, I felt a jolt of excitement. It was almost time for regular practice. Time to fly!

"Excuse me, is this elevator going up?" I asked Brooklyn, lifting my foot as if I were about to step into her hands.

I had waited through warm-ups, tapped my toe during tumbling, and sped through turns on the trampoline. Finally, it was time for stunts!

I couldn't wait to prove to Mila that I could do the elevator. But if I was the new flyer, who would replace me as a base?

Luckily, Coach Kara had it covered. She called over a blonde girl from one of the other teams. "Lily will be a base opposite you, Brooklyn," Coach explained. "You're about the same height, right? And Cassie will still be the back spot."

Lily bounded toward Brooklyn like a Labrador retriever, eager to see who was taller.

Then Mila asked loudly, "Can I work on the lib now?"

Coach shook her head. "We'll start with something basic: thigh stands. You need to get used to your new stunt groups."

I fought down a groan. Thigh stands were one of the first stunts we'd learned at cheer. I'd been practicing libs in flyer class, and now I was back to simple thigh stands? But if I had to prove to Coach that I could do the easier stunts, then that's what I would do.

Brooklyn and Lily faced each other and knelt with one knee on the mat. On Cassie's count, I put my hands on their shoulders and stepped up onto their thighs. But, whoa ... who knew their legs would feel so unsteady? I suddenly missed that panel mat from flyer class. At least it didn't wiggle under my feet! I leaned over at the waist, practically hugging Brooklyn around the neck.

She glanced up at me. "I love you, too, Joss. But you're kind of choking me."

"Oh, sorry."

"Trust your bases," said Coach Kara. The microphone around her neck sent her voice straight to my hearing aid. "It's their job to support you."

"Don't you trust me?" Brooklyn joked, batting her eyelashes.

"Of course I do," I said, laughing. But that didn't make standing on her thigh any easier.

"Lock and tighten, Joss," said Coach Kara. "Just like in flyer class, remember?"

I nodded. I closed my eyes and visualized myself standing solidly on the mat, but that made it even harder to balance.

"Let's start over," said Coach Kara after I teetered again.

"Step, lock, and tighten," Coach kept repeating. "Step, lock, tighten, and *trust*."

I tried to focus on the trust part, feeling Cassie's hands on my waist and my bases' hands holding my legs steady. Slowly, I let go of their shoulders. I raised my arms into a giant V. Then I smiled wide. I was doing it!

I almost started cheering—until I saw Mila towering above me. She was doing a thigh stand with her bases *standing* instead of kneeling. They lunged forward, their front legs bent and their knees nearly touching. And Mila didn't look the least bit unsteady. So maybe it was too soon to do a victory dance.

By the end of practice, I had graduated to a thigh stand with Brooklyn and Lily standing up, but it was a lot harder than I'd thought it would be. I kept wishing there were a solid mat beneath my feet rather than those unstable legs.

After practice, Coach Kara reminded Mila and me that we should take stunts slowly. "It would be great for Joss to work up to an elevator and you to a lib, Mila."

Mila gave an eager nod.

"But we'll do a less advanced pyramid if we need to," Coach Kara continued. "It's okay to stick with simpler stunts that we can perform well during competitions."

"But Team Fury won't be doing an easy pyramid," Mila protested. "We know they'll bring their best stunts to the competition."

I nodded. Mila and I didn't always agree on everything, but she'd been in enough competitions to know what she was talking about.

Coach shrugged. "We don't know which stunts Team Fury will do, so we can't base our routine on theirs. All we can do is our own best. Got it?"

Mila stood up tall. "I know I can do the lib," she said.

"Maybe," said Coach. "But in this pyramid, the lib depends on the elevator for stability. You both need to be stable up there."

"I'll learn the elevator," I said with all the confidence I could scrounge up. "I know I can do it. We can stick with the advanced pyramid."

When Mila flashed me a rare smile, I smiled back.

Coach Kara hesitated. "Should we invite the team to open gym on Sunday for some extra practice time?"

I nodded eagerly. I'd just promised I could do the elevator, but after wobbling my way through a thigh stand, I wasn't *totally* sure I could pull it off. This flyer needed all the practice she could get.

When I got home from cheer, I walked straight through the garage and out to the backyard. I couldn't practice flying without my stunt team, but I could run through a few tricks for the talent show—at least until the sun set.

I hopped onto the ramp with my board and carved back and forth a few times. Then I zoomed up one side and tried an ollie, kicking up my board until its wheels left the ramp. As I spun the board back around, my wheels touched down smoothly. *Nailed it!*

Sofia might be the skate trick queen, but at least I could bring *something* to the act.

When Dad let Murph into the backyard, I wondered: *Can I bring a skateboarding dog, too?* I thought of the tense look on Annika's face when she found out we might include Murph in our act. But my bulldog still hadn't skated the ramp. Was today the day?

After circling the yard, Murph waddled onto the ramp. I held my breath, waiting for her to go for my skateboard. Instead, she slumped into a heap and yawned. I pushed the board up one side of the ramp and let it roll back down.

"C'mon, Murph!" I coaxed. "Show me your skills!"

Murph watched the skateboard, but she didn't move a muscle—until it rolled too close to her. Then she jerked her paw away, leaped off the ramp, and laid down on her belly in the grass. I plopped down beside her and scratched her behind the ears. It was clear she wasn't going to skate today.

"I wish Brooklyn had never told Annika about you in the first place," I said to Murph. "That's a lot of pressure to put on a dog. And on _me_."

Murph rested her chin on her paws, so I laid back and stared at the darkening sky, my mind wandering back to cheer. _Prepare to fly. Touch the sky._ I imagined myself flying high, steady and strong, into the perfect elevator.

"Maybe you don't want to fly," I said to Murph. "But I do. I'm going to learn to fly, just like Reina. I'll do whatever it takes to help my team win."

Starting to Sweat

hen I got to the school cafeteria at lunch the next day, I found Brooklyn and Sofia at our usual table. I sat down next to Sofia and unzipped my lunch bag. Before I could even greet my friends, Annika sat down across from me.

"So, I heard your dad can do a three-sixty," she said.

"My dad?" I laughed. Dad's not much of a surfer—and whenever he steps on Dylan's old skateboard, I feel like I should pad him with bubble wrap.

"Not your dad. Your *dog*," repeated Annika.

"Oh!" The cafeteria is even noisier than the cheer gym, with chairs scraping and kids chattering all around. I finally realized what Annika was really asking. "Murph? Do a three-sixty? On a skateboard?"

She nodded. "Everyone's talking about it."

"Everyone? Who's everyone?" I glanced at Brooklyn, wondering if she had started the rumor.

Nope. She looked as baffled as I felt, and Sofia just shrugged.

Annika held out her hands. "Well, is it true? Is your

dog doing a three-sixty in the talent show?"

I hesitated. I could shut down the rumor right there and then. But Annika and her Team Fury teammates were our rivals in the talent show—and in the SoCal Spirit Challenge. So instead, I squared my shoulders. "Tell me which stunts you're doing in your talent show act," I said, "and I'll tell you what my dog is doing in ours."

I held my breath. If I knew which stunts Team Fury was doing in the talent show, I might be able to figure out how hard their stunts would be in the cheer competition, too.

Annika snorted. "Nice try," she said. "Forget I asked."

So much for that, I thought. *But I can still try to psych her out.* I smirked. "Well, then all I'll say is, yeah, it *might* be true about Murph and that three-sixty."

Annika raised an eyebrow and mumbled something I couldn't hear. Then she turned and walked away.

Brooklyn giggled. "She looked nervous."

"I'm the one who's nervous," I admitted. "Murph definitely can't do a three-sixty. In fact, she'd rather snooze on the ramp than skate on it."

"Really?" asked Sofia. "Maybe we can help you train her this weekend."

"Yes!" said Brooklyn. "I miss her cute face."

"Thanks," I said, feeling a wave of relief. "I could use your help." I held out my fists, one to Brooklyn and one to

Sofia, and they both gave me a bump.

But when lunch ended and we headed out for recess, I couldn't stop worrying: Would Murph the Amazing Skateboarding Dog *be* amazing in the talent show? Could we beat Annika and her friends? And . . . could I learn the elevator in time for the SoCal Spirit Challenge? As the California sun beat down on me, I started to sweat.

"Murph, come on," Sofia said. "Don't you want to skate?"

It was Saturday morning, and Sofia, Brooklyn, and I had just finished painting giant waves on the sides of the ramp.

But my so-called skateboarding dog still wouldn't skate on the ramp. I was starting to lose hope—the talent show was only five days away!

"Why are you being so stubborn?" I asked Murph, sitting down on the ramp beside her. When she rolled over and begged for a belly rub, Brooklyn giggled.

"Nice try," I told Murph. "Not until you skate—at least one ride!"

I dropped the skateboard onto the ramp beside her and rolled it back and forth under my foot. Murph leaped off the ramp like a shot. She paced and panted, her tongue hanging out the side of her mouth.

"What was that about?" Brooklyn asked.

I shrugged. "The last time I saw her act that way was during a thunderstorm. One clap of thunder and she ran to hide under the couch."

Sofia squinted thoughtfully. "Maybe Murph isn't being stubborn after all," she said. "Maybe she's just scared of the sound the wheels make on the ramp."

As soon as she said it, I knew she was right. I scooted off the ramp. "Oh, Murph. I'm sorry. Why didn't you say so?" I scratched her head, pressing my face against hers. "We'll figure it out, sweet girl."

"I used to be terrified of the dentist," said Sofia.

I laughed. "Yeah, I know. You still are, aren't you?"

"Hey, not so loud!" she scolded, as if the neighbors might hear. "It's embarrassing. Anyway, my dentist knows I'm scared, so he distracts me with movies while I'm getting my teeth cleaned. And he gives me coupons for fro-yo—if I survive the appointment."

"Sounds like a good dentist!" said Brooklyn.

"Yeah," I said. "But what does that have to do with Murph?"

"Maybe we need to make skating on the ramp fun for her," Sofia suggested, "by rewarding her with treats and stuff."

I nodded. It was worth a shot. "Wait here," I called as

I raced into the house. Five minutes later, I brought out a basket with all of Murph's favorite things: treats, a tug-of-war rope toy, and a chewed-up rawhide bone.

"So where do we start?" asked Brooklyn.

Sofia shrugged. "Maybe give her a treat on the ramp."

When Brooklyn shook the bag of treats and stepped onto the ramp, Murph perked up her ears. She jumped onto the ramp and sat her rump down.

"That was too easy," said Brooklyn.

"Right," I said. "Let's try getting her on the skateboard."

Brooklyn set a treat on the end of the board. Murph sniffed the air but wouldn't set a single paw on that board.

I shook the tug-of-war toy, resting one of the frayed ropes on the nose of the board. Sofia sat on the other side of the skateboard and pretended to chew on the rawhide bone, hoping Murph would leap onto the board to steal it from her. *Gross.*

But Murph only whined, pacing alongside the skateboard. That was as close as she would come to stepping on it.

If we couldn't get Murph past her fear, we'd have to cut

her from our talent show act. But everyone at school was expecting to see the Amazing Skateboarding Dog! Could we win without her?

"Let's see the thigh stand again," said Coach Kara, motioning to my group.

I sighed. It was Sunday afternoon, and my whole team had agreed to come to open gym to work on our pyramid. I was desperate to move on from thigh stands. Mila's group was already doing elevators! When Mila looked down at me from her stunt, I felt as if I were two feet tall.

I was sick and tired of "preparing to fly." If I was going to do the elevator at the competition in just three weeks, I had to start working on it *now*.

I did my best to step, lock, and tighten. I raised my arms into a high V and plastered on a smile. Then Coach Kara finally said the words I'd been longing to hear, straight from her microphone into my right ear: "Good, Joss! I think your group is ready to try the elevator."

Yes! Brooklyn gave me a fist bump. Then she whirled around and gave one to Lily and Cassie, too.

When Coach called Reina over to be an extra spotter, heat rose to my cheeks. This could either go really well, or I could completely humiliate myself in front of the best flyer at Shine Athletics.

As I put one hand on Brooklyn's shoulder and the other on Lily's, my heart thudded in my ears. On Cassie's count, I jumped up, supporting all my weight with my arms and pulling my knees to my chest. Right away, Brooklyn and Lily put their palms under my feet, and I felt Cassie's reassuring grip on my ankles.

As they dipped me down and then lifted me into the air, I felt as though I was on an actual elevator. My stomach dropped, as if that elevator were about to plunge a hundred stories. And I suddenly wanted to get off. My knees buckled.

"Straighten your legs, Joss. Trust that your bases can support you," came Coach's voice in my ear.

Straighten my legs? No way! I shifted my weight and started to rock backward and forward, trying to catch my balance.

"Lower her down," said Coach. "Let's try it again."

"You can do it, Joss," said Brooklyn as soon as my feet were safely on the floor. "Just pretend you're on a . . ." She turned away before I could catch the last word.

"A what?" I waved so that she'd look back at me.

"Pretend you're on a surfboard."

I shook my head. "That's the problem. It isn't like surfing. I keep my knees bent when I surf. Plus, you and Lily are a lot more wobbly than my surfboard!"

When a hurt look flashed across Brooklyn's face, I did some damage control. "It's not your fault," I said. "I'm just not used to it. Let's try again."

"Wait!" Reina held up her hand. "Instead of pretending you're *on* a surfboard, why don't you pretend you *are* a surfboard?"

Huh?

"Pretend your body is as stiff as a surfboard," Reina explained, "like one of those old wooden surfboards your dad turns into coffee tables."

Reina had me lie on the ground and stiffen my body from my shoulders down. Then Brooklyn lifted my feet like the handles of a wheelbarrow. While she lifted, I had to keep my back flat, my legs straight, and my knees locked until she lowered me down again.

"Be the board, Joss!" Brooklyn joked.

"I'm trying!" I answered, tightening my muscles from my shoulders down to my toes.

"Good!" said Coach. "Very good. If you do that while you're flying, you'll feel much more stable in the stunt. Let's try the elevator again."

On my next attempt, I locked my legs—stiff as a board. Stiff as a *surfboard*. But as soon as I felt unsteady, my knees buckled.

Reina waved to get my attention. "Don't look down," she said. "Keep your eyes straight ahead."

Well, I tried. I wanted to make Reina proud. But when I faltered again, my bases lowered me to the floor. *I'm letting her down*, I realized. *I'm letting all my teammates down.*

When Coach Kara offered us a water break, I hurried off the mat the way Murph slinked off the skate ramp with her tail between her legs. As I stood in line for the water fountain, Cassie tapped my shoulder. I turned to face her.

"It's tougher than it looks, isn't it?" she said.

I shrugged. "It's hard, yeah. But I'll get it."

When I turned back around, Mila had butted in line to get a drink. "Are you sure?" she asked, narrowing her eyes.

"Yes! I told you, I'll get the elevator. Don't worry about it." I turned away before Mila could respond. And when Coach Kara called us back for more stunt work, I didn't walk toward the mat. I ran.

Because time was running out.

Baby Steps

When I got home from cheer, Murph jumped onto my bed for some cuddles. I buried my face in her fur, glad to hide out there for a while.

I'd attempted the elevator several more times at practice. But no matter how much I tried to "be the board," I couldn't stand up straight for very long. And every time my team lowered me down, my hopes sank lower, too.

When Murph nestled beside me, I took out my hearing aid and put it in the case by my bed. That's when cuddle time turned into quiet time, or QT. When I'm not wearing my hearing aid, the sounds around me disappear. I can close my eyes, tune out the world, and tune in to my imagination.

I often use QT to learn a tough surf trick, going through every step in my mind until it feels like my body is really doing the moves. Liam taught me how to do that—how to visualize a move, picturing it in my mind as if I could do it perfectly. It helps my body learn the skill. I started to wonder: Could I use QT to learn the elevator?

In my mind, I pictured that elevator going up. I felt

every movement as if I were in the cheer gym with my stunt group. I visualized that stunt over and over again, until I knew I could do it. That I *would* do it, just as soon as I had the chance.

Tomorrow, I promised myself. *I'll do the elevator tomorrow.*

Monday at cheer, I stood between Brooklyn and Lily, just as I had during QT. But my sweaty palms reminded me this was no visualization. This was the real thing. Cassie was behind me with her hands on my waist, and Reina stood in front of me, ready to help spot.

On Cassie's count, I jumped up and planted my feet in my bases' palms. Cassie's hands gripped my ankles, steady and strong. *So far so good.* But that was the easy part. As my bases dipped me, preparing to hoist me up, my heartbeat ramped up, too. Because the hard part was coming.

You practiced this in QT, I reminded myself. I had visualized locking my legs and popping up into an elevator, over and over again. So as my bases lifted me into the air, I knew what to do. I let go of their shoulders and stood up straight and strong.

Am I doing it? I wondered. I looked down for only a second—and my knees instantly buckled.

"Eyes straight ahead, Joss!" said Coach Kara into her microphone. "Lock those legs!"

Brooklyn glanced up and grinned. "Be the surfboard!"

I gave her a small smile. But after another unsuccessful try, my stunt group lowered me to the ground, and my heart tanked in my chest.

Reina waved to get my attention. "Don't look down," she reminded me. "Try looking at me instead. And remember to smile."

That much, I could do. I shot Reina a grateful smile and got ready to try again.

Dip! Lock! Tighten!

I let go of my bases' shoulders and locked my legs.

Stand tall! Don't look down!

I raised my hands into a high V overhead, my body straight and strong.

This time I didn't look down. Instead, I stared straight ahead—right into Reina's eyes. I wanted to look away, afraid I'd teeter again and disappoint her. Then I remembered her advice: *Fake it till you feel it.* I flashed her my most confident smile, just like she'd taught me to do when I was trying out for cheer.

From the smile Reina gave me in return, I knew: I was doing the elevator. For real.

Reina waved her hands in the air, cheering for me the

way my family does. I smiled so hard that I thought my cheeks might crack.

From the top of the elevator, I was like a queen surveying her domain. I'd never felt so strong. Or so powerful. Or so happy.

When my bases lowered me, Brooklyn squealed. "You did it!" She pulled me into a hug.

"Nice work, Joss!" said Coach Kara.

Even Mila looked happy for me—or maybe she was just happy for herself, because now she would get to do the lib in competition. She and I could lock arms and do the more difficult pyramid. We could beat Team Fury!

"Team Fury is going down," I said, holding out my hand for our team cheer.

Mila slapped her hand on mine. "For sure," she said, her eyes flashing. "We've got this."

Brooklyn and Cassie joined in. And Lily added her hand, too, for the very first time.

As my teammates circled around, I could feel it in our fingertips—our strength and energy. I knew we could win. And a few weeks from now, we wouldn't just be practicing in this gym. We'd be *sleeping* in it to celebrate that win.

"Shhhh . . . Shine!"

Tuesday afternoon was D-day. D stood for deciding, as in deciding what our act for the talent show would be. Because now it was only two days away!

But D also stood for dog, as in the terrified bulldog in my backyard.

"We've tried pretty much everything," I said to my friends, "but Murph still won't skate the ramp. Anyone have any new ideas?"

"Can we lift her onto the skateboard on the ramp?" asked Brooklyn.

I shook my head. "That would be tough," I said. "She weighs like a trillion pounds."

"Oh, right," said Brooklyn. "If only we had a spotting rig like we do at cheer. I feel like I can do anything when I have that harness supporting me."

I stood up so fast that I almost lost my balance. "That's it, Brooks! You're a genius!"

I raced to the garage to get Murph's life vest. It's not a pulley system like the spotting rig, but it's a harness, all right. It has a handle on top, and we use it to lift Murph onto her surfboard at Dog Beach.

When I brought the life vest back into the yard, Sofia nodded. "Yeah! That could work!"

When Murph saw the life vest, she grabbed it in her mouth and tore off across the yard to the garage.

I groaned. "She thinks she's going surfing," I said.

Murph barked with joy and ran back to us, tripping over the harness with her plump paws. I quickly crouched behind her and strapped her into the life vest, which sent her rump wiggling with joy all over again. Then I pulled a skateboard out of the bin. Murph barked her approval and ran over to grab it with her mouth. She dragged it toward the driveway.

"Wrong way, Murph!" Sofia said, pointing to the ramp.

"Maybe we should just let her skate in the driveway for a few minutes," I suggested. "You know, a baby step to boost her confidence. At cheer, Coach Kara has us do an easy stunt until we feel confident enough to try a harder one—like the four million thigh stands I had to do before I could try the elevator."

"Before you *did* the elevator," Brooklyn pointed out with a grin.

My stomach fluttered just thinking about the elevator I'd pulled off at cheer last night.

As soon as Murph stepped onto the board, I waved at Brooklyn. "Go get the treats!" I said. "If we're doing the baby-step thing, we have to reward her for every tiny little step."

Brooklyn met Murph at the bottom of the driveway with a handful of treats.

"Now we've got to get her to do something more impressive." I grabbed the board and headed toward the backyard, hoping Murph would follow. When she didn't, Brooklyn made a trail of treats in the grass. Murph followed her nose, gobbling up treats along the way.

I set the skateboard on the ramp. "Now let's use the life vest to lift her onto the skateboard," I told my friends. "Or maybe just her front paws."

I led Murph over to the ramp and told her to sit. When she did, Brooklyn gave her a treat. Then I lifted one of her pudgy paws, set it on the skateboard, and gave her another treat, quick as a flash. Then we tried two paws on the board—and gave her two treats.

It took all three of us to lift Murph's backside onto the skateboard. I lifted up on the handle of her life vest just enough to let her know she was safe—that I was here. She didn't seem freaked out, but she wasn't exactly excited to take a run down the ramp either.

Slowly, slowly, slowly, we rolled the board forward a couple of inches. Murph stayed put, licking her chops as Brooklyn shook the treat bag—that was her official job now. She offered Murph a tasty morsel.

Before Murph knew what was happening, we were rolling her slowly across the ramp. I held my breath. Would she freak out if we rolled her a little faster?

Nope. She ate another treat. The next moment, she shifted her weight and I thought she was going to hop off the board. But then a miracle happened: She pushed with her paw. It was just one stroke, but it was a huge improvement.

"We did it," I cheered. "Go, Team Murph!" I put out my hand so that Sofia and Brooklyn could pile theirs on top.

By the time Brooklyn and Sofia went home, we had decided something: If our act was going to include the Amazing Skateboarding Dog, our two-girl act had to become a three-girl act. We needed Brooklyn, master dog trainer and treat giver, onstage with us.

I mean, Murph wasn't exactly ripping it up on the ramp yet. But we'd take what we could get. She had taken a few baby steps—in the right direction.

The Talent Show

H ow's this?" asked Dad. He was sliding one half of the mini ramp across the backstage area with Principal Harris.

"That's great for now," said the principal, giving Dad a thumbs-up. "Until Joss's act." The words set butterflies loose in my stomach.

It was Thursday after school, and the auditorium was packed with students and their families. The talent show was well under way, and it was almost our turn.

"Ready?" signed Sofia, who was checking the wheels of her skateboard.

Good question, I thought. In the last two days, Murph had learned how to push with her paw to get some speed on the ramp. That meant Sofia and I could sit on the decks of the ramp and roll the board down, letting Murph skate back and forth between us. If she got lazy and laid down for a nap, Brooklyn would be on Murph duty with her magical bag of treats.

"Ready as we'll ever be," I told her, leaning over to give Murph a belly rub.

Brooklyn crouched down next to me and bit her thumbnail. "I'm ready to toss my cookies," she said. "I'm so nervous, I can't [*thump, bump*]."

As Mason Anderson lugged his drum set across the backstage area, I missed Brooklyn's last few words. Murph must have heard them, though, because she got to her feet and licked Brooklyn's face.

"You'll be okay, Brooks," I said. "Murph will steal the show. All you have to do is keep the treats flowing."

She nodded, but she sure was quiet while we watched the first few fifth-grade acts. When Annika and her friends from Team Fury were up, I felt my own jolt of nervousness. One of them was a fifth-grader from Brooklyn's class, and the other two were in fourth grade. They strode onto the stage, oozing confidence with every step.

As the curtain opened and the beat of the music vibrated the floor, Annika and her friends launched into a tumbling routine. Tuck jumps, cartwheels, roundoffs—I watched their every move. I was waiting for the stunts. Would Team Fury be as good as everyone said they were?

When Annika and her friends finally set up for a stunt, I felt Sofia watching over my shoulder. Two girls faced each other as sturdy bases, and the tallest girl got ready to spot Annika from behind. As Annika stepped into their hands, I held my breath.

Would it be an elevator? *Please, please, please let it be only an elevator!*

As the bases hoisted Annika into the air, she lifted one knee, raised her arms into a high V—and popped up into a perfect lib.

I swallowed hard. As the crowd applauded and the curtains closed, I shared a knowing look with Brooklyn. Now we knew for sure that Team Fury was doing a lib in their SoCal Spirit Challenge routine. That meant our Junior One team *had* to do the elevator-lib combo or we wouldn't earn as many points for difficulty.

Good thing I finally learned the elevator, I reminded myself. But my heart fluttered in my chest.

Sofia suddenly tapped my shoulder. "We're up next!"

"Really?" My stomach clenched. Why did we have to follow Team Fury's perfect act?

I took a good hard look at my bulldog, who was sitting next to a very nervous Brooklyn. Murph was cute, but she wasn't *that* cute. We were going to have to show some real talent out there, too.

"C'mon!" Sofia waved us all toward the stage.

As Dad and Principal Harris slid the two halves of the ramp into position, I strapped on my helmet and grabbed my skateboard. Sofia and I walked onstage on shaky legs. But Murph didn't follow.

"Brooklyn?" I whispered.

Finally, Murph waddled out, her nose glued to the treat bag in Brooklyn's hand. Relief flooded my chest. *Phew!* Principal Harris gave us a thumbs-up from the wings.

As the curtains parted, light poured across the stage. I saw Mom and Dylan in the front row. Mom had taken the afternoon off from work and was waving like a wild woman. There were hundreds of people in the audience, row after row of them stretching back into the darkness.

A noise crackled over the loudspeaker—the announcer introducing our act.

I froze, my limbs suddenly heavy. Thank goodness Sofia was skating first!

She sprang into action. She hit the ramp and started pumping, rolling from one edge to the other, pulling off her famous lip tricks. Every time she paused at the top or snapped up the nose or tail of her board, she would strike a pose. And the audience ate it up. They were cheering at least as loud as they did for Team Fury, I was sure of it.

But Murph didn't seem to love the applause at all. She paced back and forth, straining at her leash. Brooklyn shot me a "what do I do?" look.

Sofia was almost done with her run, and Murph was up next. She'd be our "half-time show" before I did my ollies for the grand finale.

"Let's get Murph to the ramp," I whispered to Brooklyn. "Use the treats!"

When Brooklyn shook the bag, Murph followed her. While I set down Murph's board, Sofia climbed up one side of the ramp. I rolled the board toward Murph and climbed up the other side, hoping she would remember what to do.

She did! She hopped on the board and rolled halfway up the ramp. As it rolled back down, she pushed with a paw and got some speed. At the sight of the Amazing Skateboarding Dog, the audience erupted into applause and laughter.

Sofia and I grinned at each other. *So far, so good.*

Murph took another run, gaining speed as she careened down the ramp. I was so proud of her!

But then the audience started chanting something. What was it? Sofia held up her fingers to translate for me: *Three! Six! Zero!* Her eyes grew wide.

Uh-oh. The crowd wanted to see the Amazing Skateboarding Dog do her rumored three-sixty trick! Murph froze on the skateboard.

"Don't worry, Murph! Just keep skating!" I called.

Instead, Murph jumped off the skateboard and started pacing the ramp. She panted nervously, her tongue darting in and out of her mouth.

"Three-six-ty!" the audience chanted. "Three-six-ty!"

Murph whimpered up at me as if to say, *Get me out of here!* And I knew just how she felt.

I waved at Brooklyn, who stood frozen onstage with the treat bag. "Do something!" I cried.

Brooklyn's eyes grew wide. She turned toward the crowd and back at me. Finally, she did something—something crazy, that is. She threw the treat bag over her shoulder and started doing front walkovers across the stage!

Stop! I wanted to shout. Why was Brooklyn tumbling in the middle of our skate act?

The audience stopped chanting and started cheering. When Brooklyn reached the other side of the stage, she reversed and came right back, showing off a few back walkovers.

I tried to stop her. I stood up and waved both hands. But she just kept on going! On her third pass across the stage, she whipped off a few cartwheels. She was really catching some air now. I saw her go up for a roundoff, squeezing her legs together for the landing. But she didn't land on the stage—she landed on the skate ramp.

Boom! The sound echoed like a clap of thunder in the auditorium.

Murph cowered in fear, and then she bolted.

Right off the ramp.

Right off the stage.

As she tore down the center aisle, audience members popped out of their seats like popcorn kernels, and folding chairs toppled left and right. Murph left a wake of disaster.

When she circled back around, I leaped off the stage to try to catch her. I crouched down, bracing myself for the impact of my terrified bulldog. "Here, girl!" I cried.

But Murph didn't leap into my arms. Instead, she barreled right through me, knocking me on my butt. I looked up just in time to see her leap into Dylan's lap. His chair teetered backward as she washed his face with desperate doggy kisses.

When the audience saw that, they roared. Everywhere I looked, people were laughing and pointing.

Laughing? After we'd worked so hard to try to wow the crowd with our skate skills? Murph the Runaway Dog had pretty much stolen the talent show—and stolen my hopes of winning it, too.

So I did an escape act of my own. I ran down the dark aisle, heading straight for the exit sign. I pushed my way through the heavy auditorium doors into the bright light of the hallway, and I didn't look back.

The Wall of Shame
CHAPTER 8

I'm not going back in," I said to Sofia.

My friends had found me in the hall outside the auditorium, and that's where I was going to stay—at least until the talent show ended. I leaned against a locker, wishing I could crawl inside and hide.

"C'mon," said Sofia, tugging gently on my hand. "I think there was another act after ours, and there are places to sit now. The chairs are back up!"

I groaned, remembering how Murph had sent people to their feet and chairs toppling.

"She only knocked over a few," said Brooklyn. "It wasn't that bad!" Then she covered her face with her hands and her shoulders started shaking. Was she crying?

When I heard her snort, I realized she was laughing. "You think this is funny?" I said, my hand on my hip.

Brooklyn shook harder. Then the corners of Sofia's mouth started twitching, too.

"What is there to laugh about?" I said. "Our act was a complete and total disaster. I didn't even get to do my ollies up there."

Sofia covered her mouth, as if wiping off the smile. She mumbled something I couldn't understand.

"What?"

She moved her hand away. "I get why you're upset. I said I'd be frustrated, too, if I didn't get to do my tricks. But at least Murph skated a little—I mean, before . . . you know."

Brooklyn peeked at me through her fingers and then started laughing all over again.

When the auditorium door cracked open, Mom's blonde head poked through. "Come back inside," she signed to me. "They're announcing the winners!"

I shook my head, not ready to watch someone else win. I knew I was being a sore loser, but I couldn't help it.

Mom cast me a sympathetic smile and went back inside. Moments later, she popped her head through the door again. "Get in here," she said, signing as she spoke. "You won!"

"What?"

"C'mon! They're announcing your act!"

Sofia pretty much dragged me down the aisle and up the steps to the stage. Dylan brought Murph up, too. Good thing he had her leash, because we didn't have any more treats to bribe her with. Brooklyn had tossed them all onstage before her cheer routine. As I took a step, I felt a couple of them crunch beneath my skate shoe.

In a blur, we walked past the runners-up: Mason and

his drumsticks, and Annika and her friends, holding their red ribbons. Then Principal Harris was handing us a trophy and announcing our names into the microphone. "First place goes to Sofia Goto, Joss Kendrick, Brooklyn Tillman, and Murph the Amazing Skateboarding Dog for their, um, comedy act!"

As we posed for our picture, I couldn't even force a smile. Principal Harris's joke echoed in my head. *Comedy act?*

Instead of staring at the camera, my eyes flickered toward Annika, who looked away. It would have been the perfect moment to gloat—to lift that trophy high and do an annoying victory dance, the kind Dylan is famous for. But for some reason, I wasn't in the gloating mood. I couldn't wait to get offstage.

When we got home after the show, Dylan was in full-on Dylan mode. "I knew we'd get three Kendricks onto the Wall of Fame," he said, puffing out his chest. "I taught her everything she knows about skating, from the time she was a wee one."

"You did not teach me, Dylan. Liam did. And stop taking credit for my win." I wasn't exactly proud of our "comedy act," but I didn't want Dylan taking credit for it either.

"Huh?" Dylan raised his eyebrows. "No, I wasn't talking about you, Joss. I was talking about Murph! I can't wait to see her mug on the Wall of Fame." He held out his fingers, as if framing Murph's face for a photo.

"See?" I hollered to Mom. "He can't be serious for a single second, just like Brooklyn. They think this is a total joke. Ha, ha, ha."

Sofia had understood why I was upset, so why hadn't Brooklyn? She was a good friend, but she sure hadn't come through for me tonight. I mean, she'd done a *cheer* routine in the middle of our skate act!

I got up and started toward my bedroom. I still had cheer practice tonight and I had to change my clothes. As I passed Dad, he reached out a hand to stop me. "Hey, I know your act didn't turn out the way you hoped. But you gave those cheer girls some stiff competition. What did you call them— Team Fire?"

"Team Fury," I corrected him.

My shoulders slumped. It was true. We had done exactly what we set out to do by beating Team Fury. So . . . why didn't I feel good about it? Why didn't it *feel* like we'd won?

That night at cheer practice, I was on my game. I hit the elevator three times in a row. *Bam, bam, bam!*

"Wow," said Reina during break. "What's your secret tonight, Joss?"

I shrugged. "I'm focusing on flying tight and not looking down." I was also focusing on not talking about the talent show. My friends and I had made the Wall of Fame, all right. But it felt more like we'd scored a spot on the Wall of *Shame*.

Move on, I told myself. *Focus on cheer so that you win the **next** competition!*

But Brooklyn wasn't moving on. As we set up for our next elevator, she repeated the whole story to Cassie and Lily. "You should have seen me," she said. "I landed right on the skate ramp. But it was a pretty good roundoff, right, Joss?"

Is she actually bragging? I wondered.

"Then Murph ran off the stage," Brooklyn continued, her eyes wide. "It was kind of a catastrophe."

"Or dog-tastrophe," joked Cassie.

I let out a halfhearted chuckle, but Brooklyn burst into a fit of giggles. She didn't seem to care that *she* had scared Murph offstage, or that *she* was the reason I didn't get to do my ollies. The more I thought about it, the more frustrated I got. And that's a terrible way to go into an elevator.

When I teetered instead of standing up straight, Coach reminded me of everything I already knew. "Stand tall, eyes straight ahead," her voice rang out in my ear. "Trust your bases, Joss."

When my bases lowered me, Brooklyn cracked her old

"Don't you trust me, Joss?" joke.

But this time, I wasn't laughing. "I don't know anymore," I muttered.

"What did you say?" she asked. "You don't trust me?"

"Never mind," I said. "We can talk about it later."

Brooklyn held me to that. Right after stunt practice, she followed me off the mat. "Why did you say you don't trust me?" she asked.

My words—and frustration—spilled out. "Because you went totally rogue in the talent show. You did cheer in the middle of our skate act!"

Brooklyn's eyes got a wounded look. "You told me to do something! What was I supposed to do?"

"I don't know," I said. "Help with Murph maybe?"

Brooklyn started talking fast. "I couldn't! Murph wasn't [*mumble, mumble*] until the audience [*mumble, mumble, mumble*]. Which they wouldn't have been doing, by the way, if you hadn't told Annika that Murph could do a three-sixty."

Was she saying it was all my fault? "That rumor would never have started if you hadn't blabbed about Murph, the Amazing Skateboarding Dog!" I pointed out. "Sofia and I would have won the act with our own skateboarding skills."

"Without me, you mean?" said Brooklyn. "Right. Well,

sorry. I was just trying to help you beat Team Fury. And you know what? You did. You won, remember?"

I shook my head. "Who cares about winning?"

Wait, what? I couldn't believe those words had just come out of my mouth.

Mila, who was walking by with her gym bag, stopped in front of me. "Who cares about *winning*?" she asked. "About beating Team Fury? Um, I do. I thought you did, too, Joss."

I kicked at the mat with the toe of my shoe. "That's not what I meant. I do care about winning, but . . . I was just saying I'd rather have gotten to do my skate tricks and *lost* the talent show than win the way we did."

Brooklyn's face went blank, as if she'd pulled a curtain down to shut me out.

Mila put her hand on her hip. "So you're saying you'd rather show off your own skills than work with your team to win?"

"No!" Why did she keep twisting my words? I paused and took a deep breath. "I want to win with my team. But I need teammates I can trust."

At that, Brooklyn spun on her heel and stormed away.

Mila stared at me hard. "We do, too," she said. "Can we trust *you*, Joss?"

"Yes, you can," I snapped.

As she walked away, I stood still, my feet glued to the floor.

So much for moving on from the talent show disaster. Somehow, I'd just caused a whole new train wreck right here at cheer.

SHADOW ROCK

Saturday morning, the smell of eggs and toast drifted down the hall. *Forget breakfast*, I thought. *I couldn't eat if I tried.*

I kept going over everything that had happened on Thursday, from the start of our skateboarding act to the end of cheer practice. Then I'd rewind and play out the disaster again.

I glanced at the trophy on my desk. Sofia said it was my turn to have it, like we had shared custody or something. That ginormous trophy was proof that we had won the talent show.

So why did it feel like we'd lost?

Maybe because whenever I looked at the trophy, all I could see was Brooklyn barreling into the skate ramp and Murph bolting offstage before I got the chance to do a single ollie! We hadn't really earned the trophy, I realized. We'd just messed up and made the audience laugh, like Dylan and his dumb magic act. Maybe that was good enough for Dylan, but it wasn't good enough for me.

Of course I cared about beating Team Fury. How could Mila have doubted that? I'd learned the elevator so that we could do the more advanced stunt combination, hadn't I?

"I *do* want to win the cheer competition," I said out loud, as if Mila were standing in front of me. "But I want to win by doing our best—showing what we can do."

When my phone lit up on the nightstand, I took a quick peek. Sofia had texted.

Surf today?

Yes! The Break was where I always brought my A game. Out on the waves, it was just me and my trusty surfboard— I didn't have to rely on a stunt team to fly.

Then a shadow crept over that thought—Shadow Rock, that is. Today was Saturday, which meant Dylan and Liam were probably getting ready for their weekly surf trip right now. If I really wanted to show what I could do, I needed a real challenge. Maybe the best way to get past the talent show disaster would be to surf some amazing waves at Shadow Rock.

Dylan would say no. But could I convince Liam to say yes? I texted Sofia my plan, popped in my hearing aid, and made my way down the hall.

I found Liam and Mom in the kitchen finishing breakfast.

"What's up?" Liam signed. He used his toast to sop up runny egg yolk from his plate.

"Shadow Rock!" The words burst from my mouth. I begged Liam to take Sofia and me with him, speaking quickly before anyone could say no. "We'll be careful," I signed, looking from Mom to Liam. "*Please?*" I gave them my best puppy-dog eyes. Murph had taught me well.

Mom and Liam shared a look. "The surf report says the waves are pretty clean this morning," my brother said to Mom, signing as he spoke. "Today might be a good day to take her."

Mom paused and sipped her coffee. "Do you think she's ready?" she signed.

When Liam nodded, my belly zinged with excitement. "I think so," he signed, "but I'll make sure to watch her."

Mom held his gaze. "You'd better," she said. "Like a hawk." She used ASL to finger-spell the word: H-A-W-K. Liam was a certified lifeguard, so she knew he would keep me safe.

"Is that a yes?" I asked, looking from Mom to Liam.

Liam smiled, pointing from his eyes to mine as if he were already keeping an eye on me. "Can you be ready to go in a half hour?" he said.

"Yes!" I practically shouted.

Mom laughed. "I'll call Ms. Goto right now," she signed.

Liam followed me into the hallway. "You'd better bring your old board," he said. "Big waves plus big rocks equal big dings."

"I'm on it," I said, heading to the back door.

In the rack outside, my brand-new shortboard shone in the morning light, a swirl of pinks, blues, and yellows. Next to it stood my hand-me-down board from Dylan. It was full of repaired dings, and there was nothing shiny about it—except the loopy black autograph near the nose. *Tina Hart.* She had signed the board when I'd met her last summer.

As I grabbed that old board, I felt a jolt of confidence. It was like taking Tina with me to Shadow Rock. Things were turning around now. In an hour or two, that embarrassing talent show would be nothing but a distant memory.

As a convertible sped past Liam's van, the driver blew the horn and waved. I waved back.

"Another one?" said Sofia, laughing.

With all the attention Liam's Volkswagen bus gets from other drivers, I feel like a celebrity when I ride in it. His Surfmobile is aqua blue and decked out with racing stripes.

Inside, it's stocked with pillows, blankets, surf magazines, and snacks, just like a pop star's tour bus.

I glanced out the window. We'd been driving south along Highway 1 for half an hour, past Newport Beach and Laguna Beach. The Pacific Ocean stretched out beside us, as far as my eyes could see. I couldn't wait to be *in* that ocean, flying down the face of a killer wave. My knee started to bounce—until Dylan turned around and signed the word *finish*, telling me to stop jiggling the back of his seat. Again.

"Are you nervous or what?" he asked, shaking his hair out of his eyes.

"Nope," I said, pressing my heel to the floor.

"Well you should be," he said, signing as he spoke. "I got drilled last weekend. You should have seen the wave. It was a bone crusher. A twelve foot, for sure— probably more."

Was he trying to impress me? Or just psych me out?

Liam started in about some whopper of a wave he'd caught. Then Dylan started gesturing wildly, the waves in his own story getting bigger and bigger. I didn't catch every detail, but I didn't need to. Between Brooklyn and Annika, I'd had enough of people trying to psych each other out— just look where it had landed us in the talent show!

By the time we got to Shadow Rock, I was determined

to catch one of those big waves—something epic that would make Dylan quit the trash talking, make Brooklyn stop laughing, and make *me* feel a whole lot better about the talent show.

When Liam finally parked the van, Sofia and I tumbled out like kids springing out of bed on Christmas morning. I couldn't wait to get to the water. I could practically feel the pull of the surf down below.

The path zigzagged down a steep cliff to a rocky shoreline. I slipped and slid down the path behind Sofia, wishing I'd worn sneakers instead of sandals. Even before we reached the water, I could see that the surf was up—way up. A thick line of waves crashed around the rocky point. I'd put on my wet suit, which helps me stay warm when I surf in the fall. But still, something about the place made me shiver.

When Sofia stopped suddenly, I nearly plowed into her. She spun around. "Where is everyone?" she asked. "Do we have this break to ourselves?"

Dylan jogged to catch up. "Of course we do. No one else dares surf Shadow Rock." He nibbled his fingernails and gazed nervously out over the surf.

I pushed his shoulder. "Stop. We're not scared."

Then I saw the warning signs posted behind him— two of them. One showed a stick person falling off rocks, which looked like me slip-sliding down the trail. The other showed a stick person stuck in a rip current, waving a hand in the air for help.

When Liam came up behind us carrying a life preserver from the van, my stomach lurched. I tried to ignore it as I laid out my towel on the shore.

Beside me, Sofia stood perfectly still, gazing at the water. "How tall are those waves?" she asked Dylan.

He shaded his eyes. "Eight feet. Maybe ten."

When Sofia glanced at me, I could practically read her mind. *We're in over our heads*, she was thinking. *Literally.* "I might just . . ." The surf drowned out her words.

"What?" I studied her face.

"I might sit this set out and wait for something smaller," she said.

Liam nodded. "Good call," he said. "Trust your gut and don't go out there till you feel comfortable. How about you, Joss? Do you want to wait? It's okay if you do." When I hesitated, he signed, "Trust your gut."

I could have waited. Maybe I should have. But today was my chance to show my skills—the chance I didn't get in the talent show. So I shook my head.

Was I scared of those ginormous waves? *Yep.*

Was I going to let Dylan or even Liam see that? *Nope.*

Never let them see you sweat, I reminded myself. *You can do this. Just like you did the elevator at cheer.*

Liam squatted in front of me. "Okay, listen up," he said. "The waves here are bigger—and faster—than at the Break." He signed the words as well as spoke them, which meant he wanted me to understand every word. "You'll launch off the rocks, which can be slippery. Dylan will show you, okay?" He held my gaze until I finally nodded. "You'll need to get on your board and start paddling right away, so the waves don't push you back into the rocks. But don't paddle too far out, and be really careful coming back in."

When Liam stood back up, I flew into action before fear could get in my way. I roughed up the wax on my old board, taking a second to stare at Tina Hart's signature. *Be all in. 100%.* I'd learned that motto from Tina Hart.

I'm all in, I told myself. *Ready or not.*

Then I took out my hearing aid. As I tucked it safely in its case and wrapped the case in my towel, a part of me wanted to curl up safely in that towel, too. Instead, I gave Sofia a fist bump and followed my brothers toward the rocky takeoff point.

My first barefoot step onto the wet rocks sent a chill down my spine, but I kept going until I was standing next to Dylan. He held his board leash in his hand so it wouldn't get tangled in the rocks. When a wave surged, covering the rocks, he tossed his board straight out into the water. Then he quickly jumped in behind it and climbed on. The splash of water sprayed my bare arms, giving me goose bumps.

Dylan paddled hard, ducking under wave after wave until he was out of the white water. Then he turned and gave me a thumbs-up, as if to say, *That's how it's done.*

Liam nudged me. "Are you ready?" he signed.

I swallowed hard and nodded. As we studied the waves together, I felt like I was playing double Dutch on the playground, waiting for the right time to jump in. My heart raced.

When another wave came, Liam tapped my arm. *Now!*

I tossed my board into the water and jumped in after it.

As I plunged downward, the icy water took my breath away. My lungs contracted, and for just a second, I couldn't breathe.

The wave swept me back out toward open water. I climbed onto my board, belly down. Immediately I saw another wave heading my way.

Paddle! I reminded myself. I attacked the wave before it could push me backward into the rocks. I duck-dove under the wave, plunging the nose of my board underwater and letting the wave pass overhead. Then I surfaced and paddled again like crazy until the next wave hit.

You can do this, I told myself.

I did another duck dive, feeling the weight of that wall of water pushing me down. I popped back up, just in time to gulp down some air before the next wave came. I did another duck dive. And another. Again and again. Each time I surfaced, I paddled furiously, trying to get beyond the breaking zone before the next wave came. But these waves were so strong!

I set my sights on the water ahead, on Dylan's fire-red board and his messy mop of brown hair. *If he can make it out past the white water, you can, too,* I told myself.

And finally, I did.

By the time I reached the lineup, the calm water where I could catch my breath and wait for a wave, my arms felt like limp noodles.

Dylan was sitting on his board. His eyebrows shot up, as if he was surprised that I'd managed to paddle out through those waves. And that fired me right up. *You think that's impressive?* I wanted to say. *Wait till I catch a wave!* There were plenty of them coming my way. But, whoa, they were big. My stomach flip-flopped like a fish on a line.

I was relieved when Dylan turned his board and took the first wave, paddling to catch it. He popped to his feet and soared down the face of the wave. He made it look easy!

But I'd never surfed waves this big. They came so fast. Could I even catch one if I tried?

I caught sight of Liam standing on the rocks near Sofia. He shaded his eyes, watching my every move—my own personal lifeguard. When he gave me a thumbs-up, I felt a rush of encouragement.

When the next wave came, I turned the nose of my board toward the shore and went for it. Instantly I realized just how big—and fast—the wave was.

You're not going to make it! I could almost see Dylan's face, mocking me. *Give it up!*

But I'm no quitter. And giving up on a wave like this would mean going over the falls and getting dumped into that churning white water. *Paddle faster!* I willed my body. But my arms were numb from the cold and so tired.

When I felt the wave overtake me, I stopped paddling. I just wrapped my arms and legs around my board and held on tight.

For a few seconds, time stood still.

And then I fell, headfirst, over the falls.

Sidelined

☾ CHAPTER 10 ☽

The wave dumped me into the white water, ripping my board from my hands. My ears popped as I plunged deep underwater, tumbling head over heels. Around and around—like a rag doll in a washing machine.

When my leash tugged on my ankle, I knew my surfboard had popped to the surface. I felt a rush of relief. The wave would release me. I could swim back up. I'd be okay!

Except the wave *didn't* release me.

The turbulent water was still holding me down. I couldn't swim. I couldn't breathe. I couldn't do anything!

I'd been held under before. But never for so long. My lungs were on fire. I didn't know which way was up.

I wanted to cry—wanted Liam to come save me. But I knew Liam couldn't get to me fast enough way out here.

Don't panic, I thought. *Panicking is not an option.*

Instead, I pictured Liam's calm face, telling me what to do. *Open your eyes*, he was saying. *Look for your leash.*

I opened my eyes and reached for the leash, which was strung taut between my ankle and the surfboard on the water's surface.

Follow it to the surface, Liam told me. *Hurry!*

I took the leash in one hand, and pushed through the water with the other. Finally, I felt the pressure of the wave give way. Then I swam for my life.

When I surfaced, my lungs heaved—begging for air. I took a huge gulp and lunged for my board. I needed to grab on to something solid right now, before another wave hit and took me under.

Just as my fingers grazed the tail of the board, a wave pushed it away.

No!

I yanked the leash, as if playing tug-of-war with the surf. With one sharp tug, I closed the gap between me and my board. I used the last bit of strength I had to climb on.

I collapsed onto my board and started riding the next wave in, straight toward Sofia and Dylan, who stood together on the shore. Sofia opened her mouth—was she hollering something to me? She pointed to the right, where I saw Liam in the water with his life preserver.

Relief washed over me. I let that wave carry me, faster and faster, back toward safety.

As I got closer to shore, I realized I was coming in too fast—way too fast. Liam waved his arms, signaling me to veer right. I was heading straight for the jagged rocks!

I tried paddling backward, steering my board away from the shore. But it was too late!

As I skidded across the rocks, I saw the panic on Liam's face. I felt the rocks scrape the underside of my board.

Suddenly, my board stopped. But I didn't.

As the wave raked me across one more rock, I tried to grab hold of it. I flailed, scraping my arms and legs against the sharp surface.

Finally, the wave was done with me. It dumped me onto the rocky shoreline like a dead fish.

I laid there on my stomach, trying to catch my breath. Then Liam was beside me, his hand on my shoulder. "Are you hurt?" he signed when I glanced up.

I couldn't speak. A giant ball of emotion was stuck in my throat, threatening to burst out.

Instead of answering Liam, I wiggled my hands and feet. I pushed myself up to my hands and knees and rolled over, instantly spotting the trickles of blood running down my ankle and elbow. But all my body parts seemed to work.

I flashed back to the killer wave that had held me under, and what *could* have happened. A sob escaped my mouth— just one, but it was enough to worry Sofia.

"What hurts?" she signed, dropping beside me. "Show me!"

I pointed to my scraped-up ankle. My survival instinct

kicked in, I guess. Better to let everyone think I'd really gotten hurt than to tell them how totally freaked out I felt right now.

Dylan dropped down beside me. I waited for him to make some crack about my wipeout. But instead, he and Liam helped me off the rocks and back to the shore.

I reached for my towel, wrapping myself up tightly. As I put my hearing aid back in, my hand shook.

"That was a rogue wave," Dylan signed. "I'm surprised you took it."

I shrugged and looked away.

Liam squatted in front of me so that I could see his face. "That *was* a really big wave, Joss—too big probably," he signed as he spoke. "Remember, you have to decide for yourself what's right for you. I'm more impressed with a surfer who holds back than a surfer who attacks a wave she's not ready for and gets hurt."

He was starting to sound like Coach Kara.

"I know all that," I said in a tiny voice.

His face softened. "Okay, then. Show me what you did to yourself."

When Sofia pointed to my ankle, he examined it, turning my foot gently left and right. It wasn't turning purple, like Lauren's had, but the bloody scrapes were proof that I'd hurt myself a little.

When Liam headed to the van to find a bandage, Sofia caught my eye and offered me a fist bump. "You were pretty brave out there."

I didn't feel brave. Somehow, I had totally humiliated myself. Again. It was like watching a bad sequel to an equally bad movie: *The Talent Show Nightmare, Part Two.*

Sofia studied my face. "Were you scared?" she asked, signing the word *scared.* "That looked really scary."

I shook my head. "I'm fine." But as my throat tightened again, I looked away.

I could feel Sofia's eyes on me, as if she wanted to ask more. But instead, she sat beside me—super close, just to remind me that she was there. Then she pointed to my surfboard. "It's not cracked," she said. "Just scraped up."

I nodded.

My old board had survived the wipeout, and I had, too. So why were my hands still shaking? I hid them under my towel so that Sofia wouldn't see.

Monday at cheer, when it was time for stunt work, I was determined to get back up in that elevator and take it all the way to the top.

Enough mess-ups and wipeouts, I told myself. I would

have said it to Brooklyn, too, but she wasn't exactly talking to me. Not since Thursday night, when I'd said I didn't trust her.

Lily, on the other hand, was a chatterbox. "What happened to you?" she asked, pointing to my ankle.

I shrugged. "Surfing accident," I explained. I shot a sideways glance at Brooklyn to see if she cared about my scraped ankle as much as Lily did. But she picked at the end of her braid as if it were the most interesting thing in the world.

When Cassie had joined us and we were setting up our elevator, I got ready to step into Brooklyn's hands. As I put my hand on her shoulder, she twitched, as if trying to shake it off. *Did* she have my back?

As Brooklyn and Lily hoisted me up, my stomach clenched. Suddenly, a memory flashed across my mind. I was back at Shadow Rock, sailing over the falls headfirst. I could practically see the white water below and feel the power of the waves tugging me downward.

I panicked. My knees buckled and I grabbed Lily's shoulder—more like her head, actually. I hadn't done *that* in a long time.

"Hey!" she squealed.

Brooklyn knew something was up. She glanced at me as if I were some weird specimen that had washed up on the beach. But she didn't say a word.

"Lock those legs, Joss," said Coach Kara into her microphone. "Trust that your bases have got you."

How can I trust a base that's not speaking to me? I wanted to grumble.

I tried again, remembering everything that had worked before. I locked my legs. I kept my eyes straight ahead. But instead of seeing the back wall of the gym, I saw that wave at Shadow Rock, barreling toward me. Panic flooded my entire body.

"Joss?" said Coach Kara. Her eyes held a thousand questions. *Are you sick? Has an alien taken over your body? Did you bump your head and forget everything you learned last week?*

I wanted to tell her the truth. But if Coach Kara knew how scared I was, she might decide our group should do an easier stunt at the competition. And I already knew Team Fury would do tougher stunts. I'd seen Annika's lib!

Lily spoke up. "She hurt herself surfing." She pointed to my ankle.

"Oh, ouch," Coach said kindly. "Maybe we can work on something else today."

I nodded. "Thanks."

Then I sensed someone else watching me. Mila? I was almost afraid to look. She narrowed her eyes as if to say, *Don't you dare get hurt. Not before the SoCal Spirit Challenge.*

Suddenly, everyone in the gym seemed interested in

my ankle. "Is it sprained like Lauren's?" asked Cassie, her eyes wide.

"No!" I said. "It's not that bad." I circled my foot around to show her.

But then I thought about how quickly Coach had replaced Lauren as flyer after she'd gotten hurt.

My stomach twisted.

If I couldn't conquer my fear, would Coach Kara give me the boot, too? Would she find another, braver flyer and send me off to the sidelines with Lauren?

Elevator, Going Down

s I headed back to the cheer gym the next day, my fear rolled in like the ocean tide.

What's wrong with me? I wondered. *I haven't even stepped onto the mat yet!*

I walked with my chin up, trying to fake confidence, until Coach Kara flagged me down. She asked something I couldn't understand over the music.

"What?" I asked, turning toward her. I pulled the microphone out of my cheer backpack and handed it to her.

She mouthed the word "oh" and then quickly turned on the mic. "How's that ankle healing?" she asked again, her voice sounding loud and clear now through my hearing aid.

I waved my hand, as if the surf wipeout were a distant memory. "Much better, thank you."

"Good," she said. "Because the competition is less than two weeks away, and I want to make sure we choose the right stunts. Remember, it's not only what we do but also how we do it. If we can't do the elevator consistently, we'll need to choose something simpler, like a shoulder sit."

I swallowed hard. "Yes, Coach."

She gave me a reassuring smile. But as she walked away, that ocean tide lapped at my ankles again. Fear was closing in.

I sat down on the mat and started stretching, but I could still hear Coach Kara's voice. I spun around. She was talking to Reina a few yards away, but her voice rang out in my ear. The microphone around her neck—she had forgotten to turn it off! And she was standing so close to Reina, the microphone was picking up some of Reina's words, too.

"Joss seems off her game," Coach was saying. "If she can't get the elevator today . . ." Her voice trailed off. She sounded nervous.

"She'll get it. I'm not worried," Reina said.

I couldn't catch the rest of what she said, but I'd heard enough. My stomach clutched. Reina was going to bat for me!

I'm not worried, she had told Coach.

But *I* was.

Get it together, I scolded myself. *You can do this. Don't you dare let Reina down!*

Later, as we set up for stunts, I tried to push everything out of my mind. I didn't look at Brooklyn, and I barely spoke to chatty Lily. I just took a deep breath and waited for Cassie's count.

"Five, six, seven, eight . . ."

My body started moving. But I felt slow and clumsy.

I managed to get my feet into my bases' palms, and as they dipped me down, I squeezed my eyes shut.

Visualize the stunt, I told myself. *Just like in QT.*

Dip! Lock! Tighten! I locked my legs and squeezed them close together, stiff as a surfboard.

Look up! I opened my eyes.

Reina was there, giving me her supportive smile. I could tell by the look in her eyes that she believed in me, a hundred percent.

But that's when the memory of my wipeout at Shadow Rock came back. My legs started to shake.

Focus! I said to myself. I slowly raised my hands into a high V, trying to tighten my body. But my legs wouldn't stop shaking—not even for a second.

When Brooklyn glanced up, frustration flashed across her face, which didn't help my confidence. She said something to Cassie. Was she complaining about me?

Anger burned in the pit of my stomach, and that was all it took to bring me down.

I teetered forward and back. I flailed my arms, trying desperately to catch my balance.

And then I fell.

I stifled a scream and squeezed
my eyes shut, bracing for impact.
Then I felt my teammates' arms
beneath me—and my feet smacking
against the mat. Reina was suddenly beside me, her worried face
hovering over mine, making sure
I wasn't hurt.

Before I could catch my breath, Coach
ordered my whole team to do twenty push-ups because my
feet had hit the ground. "SPOT conditioning," she reminded
them. "Save the Person On Top. That's your job. So let's
strengthen those arms so you'll keep Joss's whole body off
the mat next time."

Brooklyn shot me a look. Even Cassie's face darkened
as she dropped to her knees to do push-ups. Why were
they mad at me? They were the ones who had let me hit
the ground!

Coach knelt next to me and Reina on the mat. "Are you
okay?" she asked.

I shook my head and tucked my knees into my chest.
I wasn't hurt, but I definitely wasn't okay. The words
tumbled out before I could think them through. "I don't
think we should do the elevator. We should do the shoulder

sit instead—at the SoCal Spirit Challenge, I mean."

Reina raised an eyebrow. "Are you sure?"

I nodded and clenched my teeth. Hot tears burned my eyes, but I held them back.

Coach Kara put her hand on my shoulder. "Thank you for your honesty, Joss. Taking a step back might be a good decision."

She squeezed my shoulder and then called my teammates over. Cassie and Lily, who were still doing push-ups, looked relieved to quit early.

But wait till they hear what Coach has to say, I thought miserably. I pushed myself up from the mat, but I kept my eyes on my cheer shoes.

Coach Kara clapped her hands to make sure everyone was listening, and then she cleared her throat. "We're going to go back to the shoulder sit and elevator combo for the competition and focus the next several practices on doing it well."

I glanced up just in time to see the confusion on Cassie's face. "But what about Team Fury?" she blurted. "There's no way we'll beat them with the easier pyramid."

I'd expected that from Mila or even from Brooklyn— but not from Cassie. It didn't really matter who said it. I knew everyone was thinking it.

"Let's not worry about Team Fury right now," said

Coach Kara. "Let's just focus on doing our best with our own stunt. That's all we can control."

Then Mila raised her hand. "Does this mean I can't do the lib?"

Coach shook her head. "Not without the elevator to stabilize you. So we'll have you do an elevator instead. But you'll still shine, Mila. Don't you worry." She gave a reassuring smile, but Mila didn't smile back. Instead, she shot daggers at me with her eyes.

During a break, I made a beeline for the water fountain. But Mila beat me to it. "Did you tell Coach you didn't want to do the elevator?" she asked, crossing her arms.

I wanted to ignore her, but how could I? She stood between me and the fountain. I finally nodded.

"You're such a *quitter*," she said, practically spitting the word. "If you're going to quit the elevator, why don't you just quit cheer?" Her face was as red as the mat beneath our feet.

Cassie and Brooklyn were behind me now. When I turned to them for help, Cassie just shrugged, and Brooklyn gave me a blank stare. She flipped the top of her water bottle open and closed, open and closed.

So pretty much my whole team wants me to quit, I realized. *No one here has my back. No one.*

When practice ended, I bolted for the gym door. I'm

pretty sure Reina called after me, but I didn't catch what she said—and I didn't want to. I pretended not to have heard her at all.

"Was that lightning?" I asked.

Mom nodded as she flipped on the windshield wipers, trying to see through the rain.

I was glad Mom was distracted by the weather. I didn't want to talk about what had just happened at cheer. If I tried, I'd start crying, for sure.

Another streak of lightning flashed across the sky—this one plain as day. Mom's fingers tightened on the steering wheel. When her phone lit up on the dashboard, she pulled over to answer it. I couldn't hear what she was saying over the sound of the rain, but I saw her face darken.

"What's wrong?" I asked when she ended the call.

Mom faced me and signed, "Dylan had Murph down at Dog Beach. She ran away when the storm hit—toward the Break."

"Oh, no!" The last time Murph had taken off during a thunderstorm, someone had found her way across town. "We have to find her!"

As Mom drove toward the beach, I squeezed my eyes

shut. *Please let Dylan find Murph,* I thought, crossing my fingers and toes. *Please, please, please.*

Finally, Mom pulled into the parking lot near the Break and reached into the backseat for her umbrella. I started to follow her out, but she stopped me.

"Stay here till the storm passes," she said firmly. "I'm just going to find Dylan and make sure he's staying safe, too."

My heart squeezed in my chest, but I knew better than to argue with Mom. Who was going to make sure Murph was safe?

I pressed my face to the window, watching Mom disappear into the darkness. Poor Murph! She was alone out there somewhere, wet and terrified.

Stay here till the storm passes, Mom had said. I glanced at the sky, watching for lightning. I counted to thirty, waiting.

Was the storm almost over? I wasn't sure. Either way, I couldn't wait anymore.

I pulled up the hood of my jacket and pushed open the car door. As I stepped outside, the rain and wind whipped against my face. I lowered my head and dashed toward the bike path that ran along the beach.

"Murph! Where are you?" I called, scanning the shadows, searching for some sign of my bulldog—a paw print, or her scared eyes glowing in the darkness.

But Murph was nowhere to be found.

I sucked in my breath and kept running.

Cold water soaked my sneakers as I sloshed into a puddle. By the time I reached the concession stand, rain was coming down sideways. I darted under the awning of the concession stand and texted Dylan:

> Did u find her yet?

His response came back instantly:

 > Nope. Still looking with Mom. Liam and Reina are searching too.

My heart sank at the sight of Reina's name. I could picture the way she had looked at me at cheer, as if I'd betrayed her or something. But I was just trying to do the right thing by choosing the shoulder sit.

My chest felt tight. I could barely breathe.

"Murph! Where are you?" I called again into the darkness.

Suddenly, I had a thought even scarier than falling from the elevator or surfing the big waves at Shadow Rock. What if we never found Murph tonight? What if we had to make lost-dog posters with our phone number at the bottom, but no one ever called? What if Murph and I never got to surf or skate goofy-footed together again? A lump the size of Murph's favorite tennis ball formed in my throat.

When a bolt of lightning lit up the sky, the hair rose on the back of my neck. *Don't panic*, I told myself. *She's out here somewhere.*

I felt the buzz of my phone in my pocket. Had Dylan found Murph?

I froze. The text was from Reina:

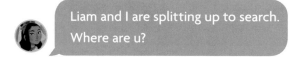

Liam and I are splitting up to search. Where are u?

I wasn't sure I was ready to see Reina. But I needed all the help I could get finding Murph. So I texted back:

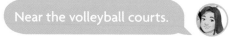

Near the volleyball courts.

As I raced past a volleyball net flapping in the wind, a rumble of thunder shook the ground. Wherever Murph was, I knew she was terrified right now. "I won't give up," I promised her. "I'll find you!"

As I neared a rack of overturned boats and paddle-boards, the skies opened up. Those sheets of rain turned into buckets, and the wind blew my hood off my head.

I did the first thing I could think of: I dropped to my knees and crawled under the boat rack.

It was as dark as midnight under there, and the ground was wet and soggy. As the mud seeped through my leggings, I didn't even care.

Because I'd just realized I wasn't alone.

A very sad, very scared bulldog was under the boat rack, too.

Hiding Out

CHAPTER 12

Murph!"

She scrambled onto my lap, drenching my face with sloppy kisses.

"Oh, poor girl!" I cried, wrapping my arms around her. "It's okay. I'm here. You're safe." Her body was shaking, so I held her tight. "I know, sweetie," I whispered. "We're the same, you and me. We get scared sometimes, don't we?" She smelled like wet socks, but I didn't mind. I buried my face in her fur and let the tears flow.

She pushed her wrinkly forehead against my hand, looking for reassurance.

"Don't worry. I'll always protect you when you're scared. I've got your back. That's what friends are for."

As I held her close for a long moment, my own words echoed in my head. *That's what friends are for.* And I thought about what had happened at cheer.

Who was going to protect me at cheer? I didn't have any friends left at practice—not a single one. No one I could count on to catch me if I fell.

I sighed and wrapped Murph in a tight hug, until

I finally felt her relax. Then I sent Mom, Dylan, Liam, and Reina a quick text to let them know I'd found Murph.

My bulldog glanced up at me with watery eyes, as if to say, *Now what?*

"I don't know, girl," I said. "I don't know what I'm going to do."

You're such a quitter, Mila had told me. But I knew that wasn't true. "Doing a shoulder sit isn't quitting, is it, Murph? I just want us to win. I don't want to fall and make a fool of myself—like we did at the talent show."

Murph gave her wet head a shake, as if I'd offended her.

"Aw, that wasn't your fault, Murph." I gave her a quick kiss. "You just got scared—because Brooklyn went off and did her own thing, and our whole act fell apart. So if my team wants to beat Team Fury in the cheer competition, we have to play it safe. Right?"

Murph set her chin on my arm and sighed. I sank down beside her and took a deep, shaky breath. I was trying to help my team win, but somehow it felt like we'd already lost.

"I'm not a quitter," I whispered to Murph. "But I sure do feel like a loser."

She gave my hand a tiny, reassuring lick.

"Thanks, girl," I said, nuzzling the scruff of her neck. At least my dog still loved me. So forget cheer. And forget the storm. Murph and I were safe in here. Maybe we'd just hide out together a little while longer.

The rain started to slow, and finally it stopped. A flash of light swept the ground beside the boat rack. Was it lightning? Murph was snoring peacefully, or as peacefully as a bulldog can snore. I waited for a rumble of thunder to jolt her awake, but it never came.

Another beam of light swept past. *A flashlight.*

"We're in here!" I cried. As I ducked my head out from under the boat rack, I saw Reina. Sofia was there, too, her wet hair plastered to her forehead.

"Is Murph in there with you?" Sofia asked.

Before I could answer, Murph crawled out from behind me and gave Sofia a slobbery greeting.

"Stop!" said Sofia, laughing. "C'mon. Let's go to the board shop and dry you off, silly girl."

As we hurried along the slippery path to the shop, I couldn't meet Reina's eyes. Would she want to talk about what had happened at cheer?

A few minutes later, we were sitting at the board shop, wrapped up in beach towels. Murph was stretched out at my feet, lapping water out of the bowl Ms. Goto had given her. Reina sat across from me. She didn't say a word about practice, but I was surprised when Sofia did.

"I heard what happened at cheer today," Sofia said. She gave me a sad smile.

Reina touched my arm. "I hope it's okay that I shared it with her, Joss. I could tell you were upset."

I took a shaky breath and nodded. "The shoulder sit is safer, that's all," I explained to Sofia. "If I can't do the elevator, we should do an easier stunt and just do it well. It's like Liam said at Shadow Rock—it's better to be safe than to take a wave I'm not ready for and get hurt."

"So you're playing it safe?" asked Sofia. She wrinkled her nose. "That's not like you, Joss. The Joss I know can do frontside airs, even if it takes her fifty tries to land one! The Joss I know tackles the biggest waves! The Joss I know is always looking for new ways to fly."

I blew out a breath of frustration. "Not anymore, not when I can't trust my cheer teammates to catch me if I fall."

Reina cocked her head. "But your teammates *did* catch you today, remember?"

"They almost dropped me!" I protested.

She hesitated. "Did you get hurt?"

I thought about the moment my feet had bounced off the mat. I hadn't gotten hurt—not really. I shook my head.

Reina gave me a sympathetic smile. "I think you can trust your team to catch you," she said. "But do you trust yourself?"

Her question caught me off guard. "Wait, what?"

She repeated it, more gently this time. "I've seen you

do the elevator," she explained. "I know you can do it. But do *you* think you can do it?"

I wanted to say yes, like I always do. *No problem! Piece of cake!*

But then I flashed back to Shadow Rock—and the big wave that had come my way. And no amount of confidence or telling myself *You can do it!* had gotten me over that wave. Instead, I'd been pummeled.

I shook my head. The truth was, I no longer trusted myself. "Not since my wipeout at Shadow Rock," I practically whispered.

Sofia's face softened. "I get it," she said. "You got banged up pretty bad."

I hung my head. "I didn't actually get hurt," I confessed. The words rolled out before I could stop them. "I was just . . . scared."

There it was. The Truth. As I spoke the words, I waited for a bolt of lightning to strike. For a tidal wave to roll in from the ocean and sweep us away. Or for Sofia and Reina to totally lose faith in me, like my teammates did at the gym.

But Sofia didn't even raise an eyebrow. She just said, "Why didn't you tell me that?"

"Because, we're Surf Sisters." I glanced at her sideways. "You know, fearless."

"Fearless, schmearless," said Sofia, waving her hand

in the air. "Everyone's scared of something."

"It's true!" said Reina. "Even Dylan and Liam."

I snorted. "They're not scared of surfing Shadow Rock. You should hear Dylan bragging about all the big waves he's caught there—and his epic wipeouts."

Reina caught my eye again. "So why do you think he talks about that stuff?"

I shrugged. "He just wants to psych me out."

"That might be part of it," Reina said with a smile. "But I think talking about scary things makes them feel *less* scary, even for Dylan."

"Surfers are always swapping stories about wipeouts down here at the Break," said Sofia.

Reina nodded. "It's a bonding thing." She leaned forward. "You may be on your own when you're surfing a big wave, Joss, but cheer is different. You're never on your own—you can trust your team to catch you if you fall. Trust is like superglue; it's the stuff that holds a team together. It's almost as important as having *fun* together."

I sighed. I couldn't remember the last time I'd had fun at cheer. Maybe it was when Brooklyn and I were eyeing up the mats, deciding where we'd sleep during the team sleepover. "Too bad we can't have our sleepover before the competition," I said, thinking out loud.

"Well . . . maybe we *can*," Reina said, her eyes shining.

I sat up straight. "Really? We could do that?"

She shrugged. "I don't know, but I'll talk to Coach about it."

The door to the board shop suddenly burst open and my brothers spilled in. Dylan shook his head like a wet dog, spraying us with droplets. Mom shook out her umbrella and stepped inside, too. "Where's that runaway bulldog?" she asked.

As Murph waddled happily toward Mom, I sighed with relief. I had confessed my fears to Sofia and Reina, and the sky hadn't fallen.

I crossed my fingers, hoping Coach Kara would let us have the sleepover this week. Because right now, I needed a little fun—and I was pretty sure my teammates did, too.

The Sleepover

After my conversation with Reina, I felt as if a huge weight had been lifted off my shoulders. Coach Kara had given her okay for the sleepover, but it didn't make Thursday night's cheer practice any easier. My teammates still weren't talking to me. And every time I tried to get Brooklyn alone, she avoided me.

So the night of the sleepover, I did what any good friend would do—I waited for her by the door to Shine Athletics so that I could ambush her on her way in.

When Brooklyn finally showed up, she started to walk right past me.

"Wait," I said, grabbing her hand. "I need to talk to you."

She pulled back her hand. When I let it go, I knew I had to talk fast.

"Brooklyn, I'm sorry!" I said right away. "For getting mad at you about the talent show. I know you were just trying to help us win with your tumbling routine."

She stared at me, looking half relieved and half frustrated. When she didn't say anything, I started to sweat.

Finally she said, "I know I didn't exactly save the day. I get that. But why'd you have to get so mad about it? I mean, we did win."

I'd figured she was going to say that, and I'd been thinking about how to answer. "I know. But it didn't feel like we won—at least not to me. I didn't get to do my ollies. It's not really a win if you don't get to do your best, is it?"

Brooklyn's face scrunched up like she wanted to argue. Finally, she just shrugged. "You're right. I'm sorry you didn't get to ..."

As a pizza delivery guy pushed through the front door, a car engine hummed outside, drowning out Brooklyn's words.

She waited until the door closed, and then she shot my words right back at me. "But wait," she said. "If it's not really winning if you don't do your best skills, then why are you bailing on the elevator for the competition?"

I swallowed hard. I hadn't seen that coming. "Because I can't do the elevator. I'll just mess it up and then—"

"You can do the elevator," she said. "I've seen you do it a bunch of times. Be honest: Why don't you want to do your best stunt?"

"Because I'm scared," I finally admitted. "Scared of falling."

"Because you don't trust me?" Brooklyn asked.

"No!" I said. "It's more like I don't trust myself. Not since my bad wipeout at Shadow Rock—the one when I scraped up my ankle, remember?"

Brooklyn nodded.

"Since then, my legs just won't lock," I explained. "You've felt me wobbling up there, Brooks. So maybe the shoulder sit *is* my best skill right now."

She took a deep breath. "Why didn't you just tell me you were scared?"

I shrugged. "You weren't exactly talking to me," I said. "But also, I didn't want to let you down. I mean, Team Fury's stunts are so good!"

Brooklyn chewed her lip. "They're good. But you're really good at stunts too, Joss. You're the only one who thinks you can't do the elevator. Everyone else knows you can." Then she pointed behind me.

I spun around and saw Cassie, Lily, Mila, and Reina in the doorway. "Hey, how long have you guys been there?" I asked, putting my hand on my hip.

"Long enough," said Reina with a smile.

Brooklyn caught my eye again. "See? Your team's got your back. I mean, as long as you don't go off making your own decisions for the team—like, you know, I did during the talent show." She gave me an apologetic smile.

Realization seeped in like water through a wet suit.

Had I gone rogue like Brooklyn had? As I glanced at Mila again, I thought of her lib, the stunt she wouldn't get to do because I'd made the decision to do the shoulder sit.

"I did kind of do that, didn't I?" I said, more to Mila than to anyone.

She shrugged. "Pretty much." But there was a twinkle in her eye.

I sighed. "I'm sorry I bailed on the elevator." I made sure everyone could hear me. "I stopped trusting myself, but I should have trusted my team. I should have asked what all of you thought. So . . . I'm sorry."

From the doorway, Reina beamed at me. You'd think I'd just nailed the elevator again or something.

I turned back to Brooklyn. "Are we okay?" I whispered.

She instantly held out her hand, palm down, for the Team Shine cheer. And she smiled.

I grinned and slapped my hand on top of hers. My teammates piled their hands on, too, for our cheer. Then we raced into the gym, the smell of pizza wafting out to greet us. Only a couple of the overhead lights were turned on, and a string of twinkly lights lit up a dinner table placed along one wall. Some of the other senior girls were setting out garlic bread and lemonade.

I filled my plate and then slid into a seat next to Lily.

"Tell us about your big wipeout at Shadow Rock. That

must have been really [*crinkle, crinkle*] . . ." she said as she opened a bag of chips.

Brooklyn elbowed her. "Joss doesn't want to talk about that," she scolded.

An awkward silence followed. I could have waited for someone to fill it, but then I thought of Dylan—trash-talking, storytelling Dylan, who wouldn't pass up this chance to bond with his buddies over his latest wipeout. So I decided to share my own story.

"It's okay. I do want to talk about it," I said.

Suddenly, all eyes were on me. Lily leaned in closer, and Cassie slid toward me on the bench. Was Mila even listening from a few feet away?

Now that I had a captive audience, I described every detail of that wipeout. I might have even exaggerated a little, just like Dylan does. "The truth is," I said, "it sort of stole my mojo. Since then, I've been kind of scared of falling. That's why I get scared when I do an elevator. It's like I can't stop seeing my wipeout."

What Mila said next nearly made me spill my lemonade: "I know exactly how you feel."

"You do?" I asked.

She nodded. "Ever since I ran into Lauren on the tumbling track, I'm freaked out about crashing into someone else. I can't even do back handsprings anymore unless the

mat is totally empty. Otherwise, I start hyperventilating."
She smiled, but her cheek twitched—so I knew she was
being honest.

Then the floodgates opened. Everyone had a scary story
to tell—except telling them didn't make us more scared.
We ended up laughing instead.

After the last story, Cassie touched my shoulder. "We
won't let you fall out of a stunt, you know. Not a chance."

"Except we kind of already did," Lily pointed out.
"My arms are still sore from all those push-ups Coach
made us do."

"Lily, shush!" said Brooklyn, giving her the eye.

I laughed out loud. "That's okay. I forgive you."

"Hey, we should practice stunts after dinner!" said
Cassie. "To help you get past your fear."

I wasn't so sure about that. "The elevator, you mean?"

"We could start with shoulder sits," said Brooklyn.
"You know, baby steps: like how we got Murph to skate
on the ramp."

I nodded, hoping baby steps would work for me, too.
So with Coach Kara's permission, my teammates and I did
some shoulder sits. Somehow, they turned into piggyback
rides. And then piggyback races!

Pretty soon, Brooklyn and I were racing Mila and
Cassie across the mat. When we accidentally bumped into

each other, we toppled to the floor. I was afraid Mila would freak out because she'd run into someone on the mat again. But instead she started giggling. We just lay sprawled on the mat, laughing until our stomachs hurt. As Mila helped me up, she said, "Hey, I'm sorry, too."

I studied her face to make sure I had heard her right. "What?"

"I should have been more patient with you," she said. "When you were learning stunts. Just saying . . ." She flashed a smile, and then she took off for the trampoline.

My jaw dropped open. "Did I hear her right?" I asked Reina, who was standing nearby. "Mila was actually being nice. And, like, supportive."

Reina shrugged. "Why wouldn't she be? She can't do well in her stunt unless you do well in yours. You're a team." She gave me a knowing smile.

When Coach Kara called us together to do trust falls, we made two circles, with one person standing in the middle of each. "Each of you will get a turn being the girl in the center," she explained. "That person will cross her arms, close her eyes, and fall backward, flying tight and trusting that her teammates will catch her. The rest of you will stand with your palms facing her. When she falls toward you, you will gently push her back up to standing before she falls again in another direction."

"I'll go first!" said Cassie. "I'm the spotter. I never get to fall."

Everyone laughed at that. It was kind of true.

So Cassie got in the middle and folded her arms across her chest. She fell toward Brooklyn, who laughed and propped her back up. Then Cassie came my way. But her knees buckled, and I had to throw out my arms to catch her.

"Fly tight, Cassie!" I reminded her. "Lock your legs— stiff as a surfboard!"

She laughed. "Good tip!"

Heat rose to my cheeks. *I just spotted our spotter,* I realized. *And she trusted me to have her back!*

Then it was my turn. Around and around I went, flying tight and trusting my teammates. It was a whole lot easier than the elevator! At least in trust falls, my feet were planted on the ground.

Later, Coach Kara turned the lights down low. "I'm heading into the office now," she said, "and the senior girls are in charge. But I need you all to make me a promise."

We fell silent. Coach sounded so serious! I studied her

face in the dim light, trying to catch every word.

Then she smiled and said, "No talking about the competition tonight. We're here to have fun. F-U-N. Got it?"

Brooklyn and I laughed at that. The really funny thing was, my teammates and I hadn't said one word about the competition since we'd gotten here!

We spread out our sleeping bags, but Brooklyn and I weren't on the panel mats like we'd thought we would be. And Mila wasn't on the trampoline. Somehow, we ended up on the same mat—all eight of our sleeping bags clustered together. Like one team.

Touching The Sky

Monday night at cheer felt different somehow. Brooklyn and Lily were joking around. Mila hung out with us during warm-ups. We even did a round of trust falls with Cassie.

When it was time to practice our routine, Coach Kara started the music, and we kicked it into gear. *We may not beat Team Fury in stunts*, I thought to myself. *We might not win at all. But we're going to work hard and wow the judges with what we **can** do.*

By the time we got to the pyramid, my body was teeming with energy—not with fear. What did I have to be afraid of? I was doing a shoulder sit, and my team had my back.

As Cassie helped me climb onto Brooklyn's shoulders, I sat up tall, popped my arms into a perfect V, and reached for Mila's hand. She reached down to me from her elevator. It wasn't the lib she was hoping for, but we both made the best of it.

I was on my game tonight, and I could feel it in every muscle of my body—every locked and tightened muscle. I was surprised when Coach Kara called us together for a talk. Had we messed up somehow?

She checked that her microphone was on. "I see a big change in all of you," she said, her voice loud and clear in my hearing aid. "Your routine is crisp. Your stunts are tight and solid. Joss, nice shoulder sit. And Mila, you made that elevator your own."

As my cheeks burned with pride, I snuck a look at Mila and was surprised to see that she looked proud, too.

"What do you think is different tonight?" Coach asked.

"We're trusting each other and working as a team?" suggested Cassie.

"And we're having fun!" I added.

Coach Kara's eyes twinkled. "Good," she said. "I'm really glad to hear that."

"Can we try the elevator?" I blurted. I guess the old Joss—Jocelyn "Confidence" Kendrick—had decided to show up. "I mean, we don't have to do it in the competition. I just want to know if we can do it. Because I think we can."

Coach Kara hesitated. "I like your use of the word *we*," she said. "So what do you think, Junior One? Should we try an elevator and a lib?"

"Yes!"

"Go, Joss!"

"Let's do it!"

I didn't hear every word, but I got the gist. My team wanted to try the tough pyramid with me. And they believed I could do it.

Reina jogged over to help spot. "Are you nervous?" she asked.

This time, I didn't lie. "Totally," I said with a smile. But I was more *excited* nervous than *scared* nervous. I shut out all thoughts of my wipeout at Shadow Rock.

Then I saw that some of Reina's senior teammates were coming over to watch. One of them started clapping the beat, encouraging us. And then they were all clapping. The whole gym was watching!

Dip and lock, I cued myself now—I didn't even need Coach Kara to remind me, especially with a whole gym of teammates clapping to support me. I rose straight and strong, with my feet in Brooklyn's and Lily's sturdy hands.

As my teammates lifted me, I felt as strong and steady as I had the day I'd first learned the elevator—when I'd soared over the gym like a queen. Before the talent show disaster. Before fighting with Brooklyn. Before getting pummeled at Shadow Rock.

Arms up. Eyes straight ahead. I picked a spot on the wall to stare at like Reina had taught me. And even when I wobbled, I didn't look down. I knew my teammates had me.

Tighten and trust. I locked my legs and smiled from ear

to ear. *This* was my best. I could feel it in every muscle of my body.

When my bases brought me down, we huddled into a group hug. Mila's group came over and added another layer to the hug. The whole gym erupted into applause.

When the noise finally died down, Lily's head popped up from the middle of our hug. "Let go!" she cried. "You guys are squishing me!"

Cassie let go and took a step back. "We *have* to do the tough pyramid at the competition." She was talking to me, but the rest of the team was listening.

My mouth went dry. I turned to Coach Kara. "Can we still do the elevator-lib combo?" I asked. "Is it too late?"

She hesitated. "Not if you can hit it consistently this week. But is that really what you want, Joss?"

I glanced at my teammates' expectant faces. "We should decide together," I said. "Team vote?"

Coach Kara nodded. "All those in favor of the tougher pyramid, raise your hands."

Mila was the first one with her hand in the air.

Brooklyn raised both hands in the air. "We should do the tougher stunts," she said.

Lily raised her hand and gave Brooklyn a high five.

Soon everyone had their hands in the air. Except for me.

When Mila's face darkened, I spoke fast. "I want to do

the elevator," I said. "I'm not afraid of falling anymore.
I know you've all got my back. But what if I'm unsteady
up there or drop the stunt and we lose the competition?
I'll be letting you all down!"

Lily cocked her head. "You're the flyer. You don't let us
down. We let *you* down," she joked.

Brooklyn laughed. "And no matter what, we'll still have
your back."

"That's right," said Cassie. "We'll all do our best, and win
or lose together."

Reina smiled. "So what do you say, Joss?"

By now, all my teammates were standing in a circle
around me. I slowly raised my hand in the air. *Yes!*

Boom, boom, boom, boom . . .

My feet buzzed with the beat of the sound system as my
team stood backstage, waiting.

"How's my bow?" I asked Brooklyn. "Is it straight?"

Brooklyn gave my bow a thumbs-up and then pointed
to her own. "Good?"

I studied the top of her head. "Pink. Sparkly. Perfectly
perfect."

"You all look fantastic!" Reina had come backstage to

give us a pep talk. "Let those matching uniforms remind you that you're in this together, okay?"

Cassie caught my eye. "Win or lose," she said with a smile.

When a backstage helper motioned for us to hit the stage, a shiver ran up my spine. *This is it!*

As we assembled on the mat, I searched the audience for my family. My eyes traveled past the judges' stand, past a group of tiny cheerleaders, and up the bleachers.

There they were! Mom, Dad, and Liam wore their Shine Athletics sweatshirts. And Dylan? He must have hit up a Halloween costume shop or something, because he was sporting a curly hot-pink clown wig.

I could have dropped dead of embarrassment right on the spot. Instead, I shook my head at Dylan and smiled. *He's just cheering me on*, I told myself. *In his own goofy way.*

When the music started, Coach Kara caught my eye and brought me back to business. She held up her fingers. *Five, six, seven, eight, and one . . .*

I dove into our routine with everything I had, every ounce of energy. I sailed through cartwheels, soared through jumps, and sparkled through dance moves. I gave it my best—for myself and for my team.

When it came time for the elevator-and-lib pyramid, I didn't even have to think.

Prepare to fly.

My body knew what to do, and I knew my team was there to help me through it.

Dip, lock, tighten, and trust.

I reached out for Mila's arm, and we rose into the air together. Up there in the elevator, with my family cheering me on and my teammates supporting me, I didn't just

prepare to fly. I flew—so high I swear I touched the sky.

A loud noise crackled in my ear. *Yikes!* The music for Team Fury was starting, and Coach Kara—with her microphone—was standing awfully close to the speakers.

Brooklyn tugged on my hand as she hurried toward the mat. I wasn't sure I wanted to watch Team Fury's routine— I'd already seen part of it during the talent show. Sure, our team had rocked our own routine. But would it be good enough?

Team Fury had more team members than we did. I counted twelve girls tumbling across the mat.

Then I spotted Annika. Cartwheels, roundoffs, walkovers, jumps—she could do it all.

But she couldn't do it alone. As she cartwheeled back
toward the center line, she found her stunt group. They
popped her up into a solid arabesque.

I could hardly breathe because I knew what was
coming next: their pyramid. My stomach clenched.

As the stunt groups set up, the gym fell silent. What
had happened to the music? I watched as a technician
rushed over to the sound board and started flipping
switches and inspecting cords.

Team Fury froze, and Brooklyn turned to me, eyes
wide. How could they pull off the rest of their routine
without music?

I watched Annika's face fall. She'd been working
so hard—I'd seen her with my own eyes at the talent
show. What if she didn't get to show off her stunts today?
I flashed back to our talent show act, which had ended
before I'd gotten to do my ollies on the skate ramp. I knew
exactly how Annika felt right now.

Suddenly, I wanted to help her. I'd done my best today—
I knew I had. Annika deserved a shot to do her best, too.

I wished I could start her stunt group back up with
a finger count, like Coach Kara does for me. *Five, six, seven,
eight, and one . . .*

But I couldn't—no one was looking my way. So I did the next best thing.

I started to clap the beat, just like the girls on the Senior team had done for me at practice.

Mila swiveled around to look at me. So did Cassie. They stared at me as if I'd gone bonkers. But then Brooklyn started clapping. And the others did, too—even Mila.

As we clapped the beat, the energy in the gym ramped back up, and so did Team Fury. The middle flyer popped up into an elevator. I waited for Annika and the other outside flyer to do their libs. But they didn't!

They did something even better: cupies.

I sucked in my breath as Annika and the other flyer flew up into elevators . . . and gasped when those elevators kept rising higher—past shoulder height, past the middle flyer—until the bases' arms were straight over their heads. *Wow!*

As Team Fury finished their routine, I couldn't help cheering for them. They'd kept going, even without music. And they'd nailed their routine.

Once all the teams had performed, we waited for the results together. When Brooklyn reached out her hand, I took it. And I reached out my other hand to Mila. Pretty soon, all eight of us were linked in a circle.

I heard the emcee announce the Junior One third-place

winners, but I didn't *really* hear it. "What did she say?"
I asked Brooklyn. "What did she say?"

"Not us!" said Brooklyn. She tilted her head so she
could hear the second-place winner.

I didn't hear that announcement either—but I didn't
need to. Brooklyn started jumping up and down. "We won
second place!" she said, squeezing my hand.

Brooklyn's jumping sent all of our linked hands bobbing
up and down, like doing "the wave" at football game. But
none of us let go—not even Mila—until it was time to walk
to the podium for our medals.

Afterward, I held out my hand for the Team Shine cheer.
We started wiggling our hands and saying "Shhhhh . . . ,"
until Coach shushed us for real so that we could hear the
announcement of the first-place winners.

"Oops!" said Brooklyn, giggling. "I forgot . . ."

She said the rest in a whisper that I couldn't make
out, but I knew just what she meant. I'd forgotten, too—that
second place wasn't first place. That another team had won.

When an announcement crackled over the loudspeaker,
I wasn't at all surprised to see Team Fury go wild. They
jumped up and down, hugging and laughing.

Team Fury streamed toward the podium to get their
medals. As they left the mat, most of the girls were still
celebrating. But Annika headed our way, toward Brooklyn

and me, carrying her team's first-place trophy.

I couldn't understand most of what she said over the noise in the gym. But I caught her last few words loud and clear. "Thank you, Joss," she said with a smile. She tipped the trophy toward me, and then hurried back to her team.

I suddenly felt about twenty-five feet tall, as if I were doing an elevator on top of an elevator on top of an elevator—especially when Reina ran over to congratulate us. "Go, Junior One!" she said. "You did great! I knew you were winners."

"Second place," Mila pointed out.

Reina shook her head. "You supported your cheer sisters, even the ones on Team Fury. There's more than one way to win top prize."

She leaned over to give me a hug. "Way to fly high, Joss," she said as she straightened back up. "I'm proud of you."

Her words sent me soaring again.

When Mila offered me a high five, I took it. Then we all clasped hands and raised them toward the sky.

Together.

 ## Cheer Terms

BASE: a person who lifts a flyer into a stunt

CUPIE: a variation of the elevator stunt in which the flyer's feet come together and the bases' arms extend overhead

ELEVATOR: a stunt in which bases hold a flyer's feet and lift her up to shoulder level

FLYER: a person who is lifted or thrown into the air in a stunt

LIB: a stunt in which the flyer stands on one foot and bends her other knee; also called a liberty

PYRAMID: two or more connected stunt groups

SCORPION: a flexibility skill that involves standing on one foot while pulling the other foot back and upward, holding it behind the head with both hands

SPOTTER: a person who helps stabilize and catch the flyer during a stunt

SPOTTING RIG: a harness suspended over a trampoline that is used to practice jumps and flips

STUNT: a skill involving lifting or tossing a flyer

STUNT STAND: a device used to practice flying positions

TOE TOUCH: a straddle jump with the hands reaching toward the toes

TUMBLING: performing gymnastic or acrobatic skills on a mat

 SKATEBOARDING TERMS

FLY RAMP: a curved skateboarding ramp; also called a quarter pipe

GOOFY-FOOTED: a skateboarder or surfer who rides with her right foot forward

LIP TRICK: a trick that involves balancing a part of the skateboard on the edge of a ramp

OLLIE: a skateboard jump performed by pushing the back foot down on the tail to launch the board into the air

THREE-SIXTY: an aerial trick where the rider and skateboard spin one full rotation

 SURF TERMS

DUCK DIVE: a maneuver where a surfer pushes her surfboard underwater and dives headfirst into a wave

FRONTSIDE AIR: an aerial trick where a surfer pushes down the tail of the surfboard and launches it off the wave

LEASH: the cord that attaches a surfer to her surfboard

LINEUP: the calm part of the ocean past the white water where surfers wait for waves

OVER THE FALLS: a wipeout where a surfer free-falls from the top of the wave into the water

WHITE WATER: the frothy, churning water created by a wave

Discussion Guide

1. After the talent show, Joss realizes that there's a difference between being *the* best and doing *her* best. How do her feelings about winning change by the end of the book?

2. Throughout the story, Joss sometimes misses parts of the conversation when there is background noise or when someone is mumbling. It can be frustrating to feel disconnected from others. Have you ever felt as if you were missing out on part of a conversation or were not being understood? How did it make you feel?

3. Joss learns that her brothers bond with other surfers by swapping stories about their wipeouts. How do things change for her when she tells her teammates about what happened at Shadow Rock? Have you ever shared your fears with a friend? Did it make you less afraid?